COLD FRONT

Novikov swore a long string of curses that encompassed *glasnost* and Soviet bureaucrats. Finally he'd exhausted his anger. He set his pipe aside and poured more vodka into the dirty glass in front of him.

If my teachers could see me now, he thought. Nearly an alcoholic, his hands tied, unable to help his motherland. And his Spetsnaz troops, once the pride of the USSR, trained to bring down the corrupt armies of the capitalists. . . . They'd been reduced to baby-sitting a pack of scientists and castoffs in the cold wasteland of Antarctica.

And all the while, an American base seemed to sit ripe for the picking, a few kilometers away.

Novikov was sure there was something strange going on at the American base. Orders or not, the major decided he was going to discover what it was.

**Harper Paperbacks by
Duncan Long**

NIGHT STALKERS

Night
STALKERS
GRIM REAPER

DUNCAN LONG

Harper Paperbacks

Harper & Row, Publishers, New York
Grand Rapids, Philadelphia, St. Louis, San Francisco
London, Singapore, Sydney, Tokyo, Toronto

This is a work of fiction. The characters, incidents, and dialogues are products of the author's imagination and are not to be construed as real. Any resemblance to actual events or persons, living or dead, is entirely coincidental.

Harper Paperbacks a division of Harper & Row, Publishers, Inc.
10 East 53rd Street, New York, N.Y. 10022

Cover art by Edwin Herder

First printing: September, 1990

Printed in the United States of America

For Jim and Tom

ACKNOWLEDGMENTS

I must extend my gratitude to those who helped me locate the technical facts, manuals, and reference books needed to obtain information about the aircraft covered in this story. Among these are James R. Bowman of United Technologies/Sikorsky Aircraft; Major Donald Riffey (US Army, Retired); SPC Russell Kirby, US Army; and Sgt. 1st Class Charlie Drake, US Army.

Many thanks to Ethan Ellenberg who came up with the original concept for this series and often acts as my private "think tank" to get me out of plot hang-ups. Thanks to my editors, Ed Breslin and Jessica Kovar, and all the folks at Harper & Row who have made another of the Night Stalkers books possible.

My usual thanks to my in-house assistants, Kristen and Nicholas, who do a good job in keeping my ego deflated. My greatest gratitude must go to my wife, Maggie, who patiently listens to the various ideas popped at her at all hours of the day. She has exorcised many "plotting bugs," typos, and other gremlins that haunted the various drafts of the manuscript.

GRIM REAPER

Major Hideki Hayashida eyed the rust caking the welds of the bulwarks he gripped. A sure sign of a loss of pride in the Japanese Imperial Navy, he mused. His gaze turned upward as the last of the balloons gracefully floated over the Indian Ocean toward the southwest. With any luck the terror balloons would reach Perth, Australia. The results would be deadly.

July 3, 1945, will mark the turning point in the war, Hayashida told himself. He studied the twenty balloons again as the prevailing westerlies carried them across the ocean. Then he turned smartly and reentered the hatch that led to the hellhole interior of the tiny Japanese sub. The stench of unwashed crewmen and diesel fuel assaulted his nostrils.

Hayashida snaked through the narrow corridor of the submarine as it sank beneath the surface of the sea with a clanging of bells and engines. He thought of how his claustrophobic existence contrasted with the free flight of the terror balloons his men had released.

His balloons were part of Japan's now frantic war effort. Heretofore, the terror balloons had been directed toward the continental US. They contained either incendiary bombs, designed to create forest fires, or antipersonnel mines, devised to demoralize the American civilians.

Thus far, Japanese Intelligence had received no confirmation that any balloons had actually reached the American mainland. But Hayashida's superiors in charge of the deployment of the war balloons believed the US Government was suppressing the information.

Japanese Intelligence did know that several large forest fires had erupted in the American Northwest. These fires were reported in the American press. Since the times of the fires coincided with the release of the terror balloons, it seemed to indicate that some incendiary balloons had reached the US mainland and had wrought real damage. Japanese Intelligence assumed that the American press was being forced to hide the facts to keep the public from panicking.

The balloons Hayashida had released today, however, were different. These new inflatables carried payloads of bacteria spores, the end result of Japan's germ warfare experiments conducted on Chinese and American prisoners of war.

As a major in Japan's Imperial Army, Hayashida had been overseeing much of the bacteria warfare research at the Pingfan Institute, forty miles south of Harbin, close to the South Manchuria Railroad. The new plague that his experimenters had created caused a fever and gradual damage to the human brain. Death came slowly, accompanied by mounting paranoia. The paranoia constrained the victim from reasoning properly or performing his assigned duties. As the highly contagious plague spread, the disorientation of both Allied troops and civilians would undoubtedly cause fighting to rage within their ranks. The Allies would battle each other, doing much of Japan's fighting for her.

Hayashida checked his gold pocket watch. Soon, his men near the Philippines would be releasing balloons from three other Japanese submarines. By the time this rusty excuse for a submarine returns me to Japan, he thought, the Allied powers will be destroying themselves, leaving their lands and possessions in the Pacific to the Empire of the Sun.

The perfect neatness of the idea appealed to Hayashida, as it had to his superiors. He reached for a cigarette and then remembered he couldn't smoke while aboard the submarine. He leaned back in his wooden chair and longed for the fresh air far above him; or better yet, his family's ornamental garden, far away in his homeland.

In the atmosphere above Hayashida, the prevailing Westerly air current wafted the twenty balloons toward Australia. Four hours later nineteen of the balloons were forced into the sea by a summer squall, sinking harmlessly into the ocean, the salt water destroying the spores.

The single balloon with an extra amount of helium in it fared better. It was driven southward by the squall flying high above the rain. Two days later it was swept through the Antarctic Convergence where the warm tropical air met the frigid air from the south. At this point the balloon was captured by the polar easterlies air current and swept southeast toward the East Antarctica Highland.

The balloon flew high over the frigid wasteland. As it dropped its altitude, the Katabatic winds sucked it inland through the Antarctic Divergence.

The cold temperatures squeezed the moisture from the air; the gale drove the terror instrument above the barren Gamburtsev Subglacial Mountains, northward to the Transantarctic Mountains that spread like a spine down the middle of the icy continent. The now-leaking balloon descended and soon the winds wedged the gasless silk bag into a rocky crevice of the Neptune Range near Mount Hawkes. The fabric of the balloon was soon covered by a blizzard of snow whipped about by the howling winds. The tin containing the deadly bacteria spores was frozen in the ice that formed around it.

Three months later Hayashida reached Japan, expecting to arrive home a hero. Instead, there was humiliation. The three submarines that were to have launched the balloons in the Philippines had been detected by the Allies and had sunk. And there was no sign that any of Hayashida's balloons had reached Australia, or that any damage had been done.

Within days of Hayashida's arrival, the Americans dropped two atomic bombs on the Japanese mainland and the Soviet Army invaded Japan. The emperor did the unthinkable: Japan surrendered.

"The Russian Army is just miles away," said Ishii, director of germ warfare research at Pingfan. Hayashida stood woodenly before his master's desk. Ishii was a thin, bespectacled Army officer in his fifties. His clean-shaven face was a mask as he poked at the bowl of sushi in front of him.

Ishii refused to meet Hayashida's eyes. The old man continued in a stolid, emotionless voice, "We must systematically destroy every piece of equipment at the Pingfan Institute. Otherwise, the Russians and Americans will undoubtedly try to blame us for the deaths of the inferior humans during our experiments. I know these people. They don't understand the ways of a warrior. They're petty, vindictive people with a false sense of superiority."

"Everything will be destroyed," Hayashida promised, speaking in the honorific style Japanese employed when addressing a superior. He clicked the heels of his leather boots sharply and bowed to his commander. He turned and left without another word, the shame of Japan's failure, and his own, causing a hot blush to creep up his neck.

Under Hayashida's direction the Imperial Army soldiers burned each scrap of incriminating material, including records of the development of spores carried on the last terror balloons three months earlier.

Soon after, Hayashida was dead. The bloody ceremonial sword lying near his body was retrieved as a souvenir by a Russian soldier dressed in a ragged uniform.

The war ended. The terror balloons that had been launched toward Australia were forgotten by the few remaining Japanese naval officers who knew of the operation.

1

The plane rested on the unlit runway that jutted into Botany Bay. The full moon cast a pale yellow glow over the United Airlines 727-22 jet. Across the bay the lights from the buildings around the Captain Cook Obelisk seemed to shimmer and dance in the dark ocean. The beacon light from the Sydney International Airport cut a white swath through the nearly cloudless sky.

The hijackers had killed one of the Americans and thrown her body from the plane. She rested on the dark tarmac, looking more like a bag of trash someone had tossed from the aircraft than a human corpse. There was little doubt among the military officers watching the proceedings that the Australian government would now be forced to either let the US troops act or to take action itself.

Captain Jefferson Davis "Oz" Carson watched impatiently from the dimly lit observation tower overlooking the runway. The observation tower had become the operations room for the elite troops and government personnel dealing with the hijackers. Oz was the head of the American Night Stalkers team that

7

the US Government had deployed to Australia at the
first hint of a crisis.

Next to Oz was Lieutenant Jim "Vic" Victor, commander of the US Army's Delta antiterrorist team that
had been dispatched with Oz. Victor was a veteran of
three previous antiterrorist missions for the US Government. The barrel-chested man had dark skin and
eyes to match. Victor's platoon would be engaged in
the ground operations needed to rescue the hostages,
if the Australians gave the Americans the go-ahead.

Oz wore a Nomax flight suit; his helmet and night-
vision goggles rested on a metal desk next to him. He
rocked forward on the balls of his feet to stretch the stiff
muscles in his long legs and wished the Australians
would take action. He studied the Australian major and
the SAS captain conversing quietly at one of the radio
consoles.

The Australian major grabbed a phone from one
of the aides who scurried around him. The major issued
an order to another aide, who quickly dashed from the
room. The SAS captain who had been speaking to
Major Bracken turned and motioned to the two Americans.

"Finally going to do something," Lieutenant Victor whispered to Oz as they ambled over to stand by
the Australian SAS officer.

"Are your men taking them or are we going to?"
Oz asked the SAS captain.

"I think we are." SAS Captain Melbourne spoke
in a thick Australian accent that contrasted sharply with
Oz's South Virginia drawl. The Australian rose and
smoothed his DPM camouflage uniform. He eyed the
two Americans and then continued, "I should qualify

that. We're going to take action *if* we can contact the prime minister. I'll bet things don't go this poorly in the US.''

"Things get snarled everywhere," Oz replied.

"Captain Melbourne," Major Bracken barked as another aide scurried from the room. "They finally found the prime minister. He's given us the go-ahead. Get your men positioned for the assault."

"Yes, sir," the SAS captain answered, donning his sand-colored beret emblazoned with a winged dagger badge.

"We'll keep the terrorists busy on the radio phone," Major Bracken continued, standing to face his captain. "In the meantime keep me informed and wait for my signal before commencing your attack. We might get lucky and get them to agree to terms. That's all. And good luck."

"Thank you, sir," the SAS captain saluted sharply, turned, and hastened through the double glass doors of the air traffic control room.

"As for you Americans"—Major Bracken turned coolly to Oz and Victor—"I think we've got everything covered here. Why don't you have your men prepare for their return trek to the States?"

"I'm afraid we're under orders to remain on alert until the hostages are freed," Oz answered. "We'd like to stay here if possible."

"As you wish." The major smiled. He stroked his handlebar mustache for a moment, then continued: "You're not in the way here. But my men will have your people in that plane freed in short order. Look at where those fool terrorists have parked the plane."

Oz studied the dark runway for the thousandth

time as the SAS major swaggered away. The 727 was resting on the north/south runway extending into Botany Bay; the plane was surrounded on three sides by water.

Little was known about the antinuclear terrorists holding the plane; they were disturbed that the new Australian government had announced its plans to allow US Navy ships carrying nuclear weapons to dock at Australian ports. The terrorists were trying to put an end to this policy.

The hijackers claimed to have nuclear material wrapped around sticks of dynamite. If their conditions weren't met, they threatened to explode their crude bomb. It wouldn't be a big explosion; there was no danger of the nuclear material causing an atomic chain reaction. But the debris from the explosion would be filled with radioactive waste that would rain down on the city of Sydney. That had the Australian authorities just as worried as the possibility of losing the passengers aboard the plane.

"You think they really have a bomb aboard?" Oz asked Victor quietly as the two gazed at the aircraft through the wide plate-glass window.

Victor tugged at the strap on his combat vest. "The three hostages the terrorists released said they did."

"But do you think they really have nuclear materials?" Oz persisted. "What's your gut tell you?"

Victor continued gazing at the darkened aircraft. "I don't think they do," he said finally. "Even nuclear waste would be hard to get and handle. I know we have to operate as if they have the nuke waste and dynamite. But I'm betting they only have firearms and maybe hand grenades."

"That's my bet, too," Oz responded. "But heaven help us if they do have such a device."

Victor glanced toward the Australian major to be sure he was out of earshot. The officer was speaking quietly into a telephone. "I hope the Aussies know what they're doing. Look at the positioning of the airplane on the airstrip. The only clear approach to the plane is down the open runway."

"Or from the ocean."

"Yeah. But look at that embankment. I wish we could have tried the Oz Proposal."

"Plan K," Oz corrected the lieutenant with a smile. Oz had devised the maneuver but it had been honed by his helicopter crew and the Delta Team. He preferred not to call it "the Oz Proposal" because he didn't feel that the credit was all his. As far as he was concerned, it had been a team effort.

"Plan K's just what's needed here," Victor continued. "Walking down the runway or climbing out of the ocean is not going to work if the hijackers have any smarts at all."

"What the bloody hell are they doing now?" Major Bracken exploded, jumping from his chair so hastily he nearly knocked it over.

On the runway the jet plane's engines were coming to life.

"I thought they didn't have enough fuel for take-off," the major yelled. "Is our information that far off!"

"I think they're turning around," Oz said.

The plane's nose had been pointed toward the bay. Now the pilot was swinging the aircraft around so it faced the airport, its tail toward the ocean. The engines were cut and their noise whirred to a stop.

The major finally spoke. "By God, they're covering the runway with the landing lights." Unconsciously he rubbed his palms together. "They're playing right into our hands," he exalted. "They've left their rear—and the jet's blind spot—toward the bay." The major rushed to the nearby desk and snatched the phone.

"Can these terrorists be that dumb?" Victor asked Oz in a low voice.

"Let me see your binoculars," Oz told the American lieutenant. He took the binoculars from Victor and lifted them to his eyes. "I bet you anything the hijackers have got men on the ground. There's a lot of brush along the runway. They must have a reason for leaving the rear of the plane exposed like that. Check the right of the runway, Lieutenant. The SAS is coming in two—no, three—rubber dinghies." Oz handed the binoculars back to Lieutenant Victor.

"Yeah, I see them," Victor said as he peered through the binoculars. "Damn, they're exposed out there on the water! Especially with this full moon."

"The terrs refuse to answer the radio," the major announced to the room. "I guess our negotiations have officially broken down. Call the prime minister and tell him we're going in," he told an aide as he stood and crossed the room to stand by Oz. "I'm giving my men the green light. Watch the runway to the rear of the plane."

Oz could barely discern the second rubber dinghy as it neared the edge of the tarmac. He watched as a squad of shadowy figures clamored from the ocean onto the sandy bank and blended into the tall grass and bushes.

*   *   *

In the brush alongside the runway below Oz, SAS Captain Melbourne whispered into his radio, "We're in position. Request confirmation."

"Confirmation affirmative," Major Bracken's voice came back on the radio.

Captain Melbourne scanned the runway. His men in the second team opposite him should be in position, even though he couldn't see them. "Power House, are you ready?" he asked over the radio.

"Pow'r 'ouse ready," a thick Australian accent crackled on the radio.

"Power House, go in thirty seconds."

"Pow'r 'ouse going in thirty," Melbourne's sergeant replied, the transmission ending with a burst of static. The sergeant's shadowy figure, along with the five men under his command, scrambled over the edge of the runway. Then they crouched, waiting with their Steyr AUG bullpup rifles.

"Cover us," Melbourne ordered the sniper next to him. "Don't fire unless you receive orders or the terrs start firing."

"Yes, sir." The sniper crept onto the edge of the runway, dropped to his knees, and set his AUG H-Bar on its bipod. The soldier assumed a prone position behind his automatic rifle and sighted through the night-vision scope mounted on the weapon. There was a soft snap as his forefinger pushed the cross-bolt safety in back of the trigger into its fire position.

The waves softly lapped at the sand. Then a distant jet on the opposite end of the airport started to gun its engines as it prepared for takeoff.

Captain Melbourne took a deep breath before speaking: "That's thirty seconds. The rest of you follow me. This is it." He clicked the safety of his AUG and scuttled through the brush and sand onto the concrete runway.

The soldiers jogged toward the plane, their boots clattering noisily on the pavement. The moonlit shadows of the SAS troops chased alongside them like dark phantoms.

Melbourne's breath, streaming through his mouth and nostrils, seemed to him to be creating enough noise to wake those sleeping across the bay. Melbourne had the uneasy feeling they were being watched.

"Pow'r One," the voice of Melbourne's sergeant spoke through the tiny earpiece. "Something's not right."

Melbourne slowed his pace, shifted his rifle to one hand, and fished the radio awkwardly from his pocket. "Continue to advance, Power House," he ordered the second group of men.

"Yes, sir. But something's—"

The twin blasts of claymore mines ripped through the night. With the blast Melbourne felt the sharp cutting of ball-bearing shrapnel from the two explosions.

The terrorists had skillfully set the two claymores. The wide, overlapping swaths of destruction blanketed the two columns of SAS troops approaching the rear of the plane. The projectiles raised a spray in the ocean on either side of the runway as the SAS troops dropped to the concrete.

"Melbourne! What's going on down there?" Major Bracken called from the air traffic control tower. "Melbourne?"

The question went unanswered. Melbourne's lifeless eyes gazed at the night sky, a trickle of blood running from the corner of his lips. The entire SAS platoon lay around him, motionless in pools of blood.

"The radio telephone, sir," an aide informed the shaken major standing in the observation tower.

"Uh, yes," the major said. "Put it on the speaker."

The speakers in the tower crackled to life. "That was very stuipd," the voice said. "Don't try it again. We have the whole runway booby-trapped. We'll be dumping two additional American bodies to help you remember to mind your P's and Q's. We'll be ready to talk again in a half hour. You'd better have something to give us by then or we're going to get serious. One hostage killed every five minutes and then we blow our bomb in an hour if our demands aren't met."

The radio channel hissed as the message ended.

Major Bracken crossed to the console and slumped into a chair. Then he regained control of himself and turned to one of the phones sitting beside him. He dialed a number as two dark shapes were dumped from the entry door of the 727 onto the tarmac.

The major spoke into the phone for several minutes. Then he hung up, stood, and crossed the room to Oz and Victor. Even in the dim light, Oz could see the major's face was ashen.

"My government has agreed to let your Delta Team try to storm the plane," the major murmured in a low voice. "But, frankly, I don't see what you can do. You'll have"—he glanced at his watch—"twenty-eight minutes. If you can't do anything by then, the prime minister is prepared to make concessions."

"I'll need help from the air traffic controller," Oz said.

"That shouldn't be necessary," the major objected. "All traffic's been rerouted around—"

"I need to talk to air traffic control, now," Oz repeated.

"Sure. Right away," the major said, nodding, the fight gone from him.

"And it would be good if we could have a bomb squad standing by," Oz continued. "There'll likely be unexploded booby traps on the field after we free the hostages."

"I'll take care of it," Major Bracken replied. He motioned to his aide and ordered him to get air traffic control on the phone.

While the major was talking on the phone, Oz gave quick instructions to his own flight crew via the portable radio he carried on his belt. Then he quickly explained his plan to Victor.

"So we finally try the, uh, Plan K?" Victor asked.

Oz nodded grimly. He'd have liked to have had time to perfect it at Fort Bragg. But it was the only tactic that might succeed in the situation they now faced. They had little choice but to employ it.

He glanced through the large plate-glass window of the observation tower. The fifteen dark shapes lying on the runway reminded him of how dangerous the job would be. His blue eyes studied the tarmac a moment, and then he rubbed the back of his head. Under his close-cropped blond hair, he could feel the scar where the three-inch piece of shrapnel had pierced his flight helmet and skull during his tour of duty in Vietnam. The plastic plate still felt like a foreign object.

Enough worrying, Oz chided himself.

It was time to get to work.

2

Oz held his black, sixty-four-foot MH-60K helicopter suspended a few meters above the gently rolling ocean. The water shimmered in the wash from the chopper's blades. The moon was setting behind the brightly lit Sydney skyscrapers, leaving the snippets of clouds tinted in yellow and orange.

As the air mission commander, Oz had full control of the operation. In addition to his chopper, two more MH-60K SOA helicopters identical to the one he flew waited at the airport. One would assist him after the rescue attempt was launched against the 727. The other would remain in reserve to deal with any unexpected events on the part of the terrorists.

"Weapons are armed," Oz's copilot, Lt. Chad Norton, said. Known as "Death Song" to his friends, Norton was a skilled navigator and gunner. Beneath his night-vision goggles, his dark face and tomahawk nose proclaimed his American Indian ancestry.

Oz eyed the heaving, swirling water below him and then glanced at the jet aircraft on the runway ahead, pursing his narrow lips in thought. Everything he saw was painted in varying shades of green and white by his NVG. "O.T., how're you guys doing back there?" he asked his warrant officer.

Lt. Harvey Litwin's reply crackled on the intercom, "We've got our Miniguns primed and powered." Litwin rode on the other side of the partition behind Oz on the left of the crew compartment. His handle was O.T.—short for "Old Timer." He was easily the oldest man on the MH-60K and had served three tours of duty in Vietnam.

"We're ready," SP4 Mike Luger concurred over the intercom. Luger felt tense about the mission ahead. He had the body of a jogger and at the moment his muscles were so tight they seemed to twitch with nervous energy. In sharp contrast to O.T., Luger was the youngest man aboard—and looked even younger than his twenty years.

Each of the four Night Stalkers wore olive-green Nomax suits, their heads encased in olive-green helmets. Each helmet was emblazoned with the logo of its owner's "handle." Like Oz and Death Song, the two gunners wore visored night-vision goggles fastened to rubber straps extending around the back of their helmets.

"Lieutenant Victor," Oz said over the intercom. "How is it back there?"

In the passenger compartment Lieutenant Victor answered, "Ready and waiting."

"Shouldn't have to wait much longer," Oz said. "The first jet should be flying by soon."

Victor turned to his men who surrounded him in the darkness. The squad of Delta Force troopers sat grimly in the folding chairs in the passenger section of the MH-60K. Each was secured in his seat by a shoulder harness to keep him from being thrown around if the helicopter executed any violent maneuvers.

The soldiers wore black stocking caps rather than the standard Kevlar "Fritz" helmets in order to reduce the possibility of noise before their attack. All wore camouflaged vests with a wealth of pockets and Kevlar armor integrated into the fabric.

Armament for each of the eleven Delta Team members was varied according to his duties. Four carried carbine versions of the Colt M16-A2 rifle like that held by Victor; three were armed with similar carbines chambered for a heavy 9mm cartridge, coupled with integral silencers built into the handguards of the short weapons. Both types of rifles had electric-dot Aimpoint scopes mounted in their carrying handles. Two of the other soldiers bore M203 grenade launchers loaded with tear gas cartridges. One soldier grasped a Minimi machine gun. All carried stun and tear gas grenades on their vests and each had a fighting knife of his own choosing.

Half the platoon was equipped with night-vision goggles; each soldier had a gas mask strapped to his leg and two had packs of special equipment on their backs. All wore black running shoes to minimize noise when the mission began.

Victor and the team leaders wore miniature radios under their stocking caps; an earphone covered one ear and the mike extended around each man's cheek. The miniature radios enabled them to have hands-free communication and eliminated committing one man to operating a large backpack radio.

The MH-60K helicopter was armed to the hilt, with external tank suite struts that had been modified to carry four pods on a standard NATO rack system. On the right side of the rack was a pod containing double 7.62mm machine guns. Next to it was a twelve-tube 2.75-inch rocket launcher pod. On its left the helicopter hauled a special jamming pod that, when activated, would blanket the two radio frequencies being used by the terrorists with static. Its sister pod contained special electronics, jokingly referred to as the "stereo" because of their resemblance to the components of a stereo system. Additional armament was found in the 7.62mm, six-barreled Miniguns mounted in the gunner's door, located on each side of the chopper; these were manned by O.T. and Luger.

"America One?" The air traffic controller's Australian accent cut in on Oz's radio.

"Reading you loud and clear, Air Traffic Control. Over," Oz answered.

"Our next bird will pass over you in . . . fifteen seconds. Over."

"Roger, over and out." In accordance with Oz's request, air traffic control was routing incoming jets as close as possible above the runway where the hijackers were parked.

Oz spoke to his crew and his passengers. "Hang on, we're heading in. Death Song, hit the 'stereo' and start jamming the terrorists' frequencies."

The copilot switched on the two special pods. "Stereo and jamming on."

The jamming would keep any terrorists stationed outside the plane from warning their comrades over hand-held radios if they should spot the dark American chopper.

In operation, the "stereo" miked the MH-60K's

twin power plant and rotors, creating an inverted analog of the sound, which amplified and then blasted from the speakers of the unit. The stereo thus canceled out much of the original engine and blade noise. While the stereo wasn't capable of completely dampening the din of the MH-60K, it decreased it to the point that it could be hidden under the thundering noise of the jet airliner that would be passing above the runway. With any luck the stereo would make it possible to execute Plan K without the terrorists inside the 727 being aware of the American helicopter's approach.

"Can you see the jet back there?" the pilot asked his crew.

"I see its landing lights," O.T. answered. "Here it comes. It's almost above us."

Oz pulled upward on the collective pitch lever in his left hand. The MH-60K responded smoothly in a brisk maneuver that enabled the aircraft to swiftly climb ten meters higher.

As the helicopter leapt, Oz depressed his left rudder pedal slightly to compensate for the crosswind from the bay and nudged the control column forward. The MH-60K bounded forward as the shadowy figure of a 747 hurtled loudly overhead.

Oz sped toward the tail of the aircraft held by the terrorists.

"There's a hijacker east of the tail of the jet, in the tall brush," O.T. warned.

"My man's got him," Victor called over his headset radio.

One of the Delta troopers fired from the open side door; there was a brief crackling from his silenced AR-15 carbine. From his side window Oz saw the dark form of the hijacker drop to the ground as the 9mm slugs tore into him.

That's for the SAS soldiers, Oz thought grimly to himself as he lifted the chopper aloft, seeming to almost scrape the tail fin of the 727.

"There's no radio traffic getting in or out of the plane," Death Song informed Oz in a monotone.

"Are we about there, O.T.?" Oz asked, slowing the chopper so it hung over the tail of the jet.

O.T. scrutinized the plane from the gunner's door. "Forward about four feet."

Oz nudged the control column forward, then held it in its center position again.

"Good! Hold it there," O.T. ordered.

"It's all yours, Lieutenant Victor," Oz said over the radio, which was still patched into his system.

"We're heading down!" Victor answered, giving hand signals to his first team. The soldiers quickly took their positions along the doors of the helicopter.

Oz gripped the collective pitch lever, ready to compensate for the change in weight after the troops had descended to the jet. Oz watched the glowing forward-looking infrared screen on his console. "Still no sign of anyone else on the ground around the plane," he told Victor and the helicopter crew.

As the MH-60K hovered above the 727, Lieutenant Victor and five of his eleven-man Delta squad rappeled from the "fast rope" bar attached above the door of the chopper. They swiftly slid into the darkness to land on the left and right engine pylon fairing.

The soldiers rappeled with their weapons slung across their backs. They landed on the pylon in a crouch, taking care to keep their balance as they released the nylon cords they'd slid down on. Four of them immediately began deploying the special equipment designed for executing Plan K.

"American One, this is Air Traffic Control," an Australian voice broke in on the radio. "We'll have another arrival over your position in fifty seconds."

"That's a roger, Air Traffic Control," Oz replied. He then switched to the Delta Team's radio frequency. "Lieutenant Victor, we have fifty seconds until another bird comes over."

"I'm copying you. We should make it."

The lead soldier on each pylon extended a folding ladder he'd removed from his backpack. The spidery device was snaked up the side of the plane. The ladders were positioned so their tops were over the roof above the restrooms inside the rear of the jet. Once positioned, each man listened as the roar of the incoming jet filled the night sky.

"Ready," Victor said.

Each soldier depressed a button that armed a series of explosives in the ladder.

"Now!" Victor shouted above the din of the jet airplane passing overhead.

The soldiers pushed the firing buttons on the ladders. Tiny explosive charges ignited in the ladders, their sounds muffled by the metal seals that contained them. With smacking sounds, the explosions drove bolts from the ladders into the rib bracing of the 727.

Victor watched as the explosive bolts of the ladder in front of him snapped into place on the starboard of the plane. He felt sweat break out on the back of his neck as he wondered if the sound had been detected by those inside the jet. Were the hostages being killed right this moment because of the noise of the ladders? he asked himself. Then he pushed the worry from his mind. He couldn't afford to let such thoughts interfere with his work.

The soldiers who had fastened the ladders to the plane clamored up the devices. Working as carefully as a team of surgeons, each removed a tool and pressed it against the hull. With quick twists the instruments' titanium blades cut holes through the thin skin of the craft. Both soldiers then quickly pushed a fiber optic viewer into the holes they'd created. Using the remote eyes, the troopers examined the interior of the restrooms.

Victor watched tensely as he balanced on the engine cowling.

"Starboard restroom is clear," one soldier declared over the radio.

"Port restroom's clear, too."

"Get the can openers," Victor ordered his men over the radio.

The two soldiers extracted tools that resembled short spades from their backpacks. The aluminum and titanium tools were carefully positioned above the restrooms and forced through the thin skin of the hull like giant can openers. The soldiers worked the tools with the skill that came from long hours of practice, rapidly cutting a jagged line that would soon form two new entrances into the plane.

"The restrooms are clear," Victor announced over his radio. "We'll be inside in just a few seconds."

"Roger," Oz said. "Hang on a few more minutes. I'm going to get American Two into position for the diversion." The pilot switched channels on his radio into the ABN/UHF frequency.

"American Two," Oz said to the pilot in the second MH-60K helicopter waiting in the distance. "Stand by to advance on my signal."

"American Two waiting for your signal to advance."

"We have another jet passing by," the air traffic controller warned.

"Roger," Oz said as he eased forward on the control column. The shadowy form of his helicopter inched forward as another large plane thundered overhead, masking—the pilot prayed—the slightly greater sound of his helicopter as it moved.

"O.T.," Oz called on the intercom. "First-class seating is about a meter and a half behind the front entry door. Back a couple of view ports from the door. Can you see it?"

"I've spotted the position," O.T. said as he leaned out his gun port. "Stop. We're right above it."

Oz again centered the control column and adjusted the collective pitch lever so they hovered above the 727 airliner. He knew this would be the most perilous part of the operation. The hostages released earlier had revealed that the passengers and flight attendants had been herded into tourist-class seating at the center of the plane. First class was being used by the terrorists. Therefore, the next four Delta troops to rappel down would be landing on the skin of the plane above the terrorists.

Oz switched to the Delta radio frequency. "We're positioned."

"Team two, come on down," Victor ordered his men.

The five Delta troopers slid silently down their nylon rappeling lines. As they neared the hull they checked their speed and slowly eased the last few feet to the plane as another jet thundered overhead. The soldiers carefully balanced on all fours as they noiselessly settled onto the skin of the 727.

The four troopers instantly pulled special stun grenade launchers that were built like antitank warheads. They placed the funnel-shaped muzzles of the launchers against the top surface of the hull.

The team leader inspected the positioning of the men kneeling on the hull around him. Satisfied, he turned and gave Victor a thumbs-up signal.

"We're ready," Victor radioed Oz.

Oz switched his radio into the ABN/UHF channel again, connecting the pilot to the second MH-60K helicopter waiting in the distance. "American Two, come on in."

"American Two moving to our second position."

"American Three," Oz continued. "Come in to about six hundred meters and sit tight."

"American Three moving forward to six hundred meters from objective."

"Luger, get ready," Oz ordered, shoving the control column to the left to nudge his chopper to the port of the 727. Rather than hit a rudder to turn the nose of the MH-60K toward the jet, he kept his starboard parallel to the passenger jet. This would give Luger a clear shot at the 727's door and—given the greater accuracy of the Minigun—reduce the chances of accidentally injuring a hostage.

"American Two, switch on your landing light and drop down into the 727's beams," Oz ordered. "Do not return fire or hold your position if they start shooting at you. You're just a temporary decoy."

"Roger," the pilot of the American Two MH-60K replied.

Oz switched to the Delta Force's frequency. "Lieutenant Victor, let's do it."

"That's a roger down here."

The landing light on the American Two helicopter came on as it dropped into the beams of light projecting from the 727 jet. To anyone in the 727's cockpit, the black Army chopper would appear to have materialized from thin air only fifty feet away.

The results were almost immediate.

"Front entry door's cracking open," Luger warned.

"Wait for Victor before firing!" Oz ordered. With alarm he saw the side door of the jet swing ajar. How long before they see us rather than the decoy ahead of the plane? Oz wondered. What was holding Victor up?

As if to answer his question, Lieutenant Victor called over the radio, "On three. One . . . Two . . . Three!"

Four explosions ripped through the hull into the jet's first-class passenger compartment. Hot gas and metal streamed in with the blasts, rocking the interior of the compartment and momentarily stunning the four terrorists inside the chamber.

With the blasts Luger fired the Minigun. The weapon exploded in a ragged, whirring explosion of sound as a ten-round burst cut into the hijacker who was now sticking a hunting rifle out the door. The man fell to the tarmac, swinging the door wide open with his fall.

"We'll hold position, Luger," Oz called on the intercom. "Keep a sharp eye on the doorway." The pilot then spoke over the radio, "American Two, back off to six hundred yards so you're not caught in our fire."

"Roger." The chopper lifted in a tight turn and vanished in the darkness.

At the rear of the 727, Victor and his four men had slipped through the holes cut into the restrooms as the blasts erupted over first class. As they burst from the restrooms, his troopers tossed stun grenades down the narrow aisle in front of them. The grenades burst with brilliant flashes, creating a stunning concussion without throwing any dangerous shrapnel. The blasts were accompanied by the screams of frightened passengers.

"Everyone down!" Victor thundered, as he had a hundred times before during training. Anyone who didn't get down or who carried a weapon was considered the enemy. The Delta troops were trained to shoot such people instantly; soldiers fired by reflex rather than trying to sort out friend from foe.

Victor headed down the aisle. He could hear the soldier behind him rip open the storage closet next to the restroom on the port side, keeping it covered with his carbine.

Victor wasted no time. He charged down the narrow aisle toward the cockpit of the plane.

A voice cried from a row of seats behind him, "You American bastards!"

A muffled burst erupted from the silenced carbine of the Delta soldier who guarded the port side of the passenger compartment. Victor didn't turn to see what had happened, keeping his eyes focused on the blue curtain pulled across the aisle ahead of him. He knew the three soldiers behind him would guard the passengers, watching for any "changelings"—terrorists posing as hostages.

As Victor continued forward a bearded giant pushed through the curtains at the rear of the first-class passenger compartment. The American lieutenant reacted before his mind was even aware of the giant's revolver. Victor's carbine sputtered a three-round burst that was deafening within the confines of the plane.

The enormous ruffian spun about, spastically grabbing at the blue curtain and raising his revolver.

Victor fired another burst. The cloth supported the giant's weight for another moment, then gave way with a rending sound. The thug crashed to the floor.

Almost before the curtain was ripped away, Victor and the Delta soldier who was now alongside him fired at the two armed terrorists suddenly exposed by the falling cloth.

The hijackers had recovered from the blast they'd received earlier through the ceiling of the plane. Now they brought up their weapons.

Victor's slugs stitched across one hijacker's face and the man's head cracked apart. The other terrorist clutched his chest. As a second burst of slugs from the soldier beside Victor struck him, he dropped his gun and fell.

Victor continued to watch the front of the plane as he advanced. Another gunman peered around one of the large first-class recliners, a glint of light reflecting from his weapon's barrel barely discernible over the top of the seat.

Victor stitched the recliner with a three-round burst from his rifle. To his amazement, the man bounded across the narrow aisle and tumbled from the front entry door.

Outside in the MH-60K helicopter, Luger saw the Australian F1 submachine gun the terrorist carried and prepared to fire, taking care not to hit the four Delta troopers still atop the airplane above the first-class compartment.

Luger hesitated too long. The sputtering flame from the Minigun missed the terrorist as he leapt through the doorway a fraction of a second before the burst from the helicopter's gun tore apart the door frame.

"One's getting away," Victor yelled over his radio.

"We'll get him," Oz said, goosing the chopper to follow the terrorist, who was running toward the ocean at the boundary of the runway.

"Think he knows where the booby traps are?" Death Song said as they gained on the lone man.

"I'll stay several meters above the ground, in case he's forgotten," Oz said.

"Don't fire through the doorway," Victor said over the radio. "We're going forward to the cockpit."

"We'll hold our fire at the plane unless requested to do otherwise," Oz replied. He then pulled the helicopter into the air, leapfrogging the running terrorist. Oz kicked the left rudder pedal to swing the tail of the chopper around in a giddy circle so he faced the terrorist, cutting off his escape route into the ocean. The pilot snapped on the landing light, bathing the man in a blinding cone of brightness.

The hijacker froze. For a second Oz thought the man was going to surrender. Then, with little warning, the terrorist raised his submachine gun and fired a long burst at the helicopter.

Oz ignored the 9mm projectiles crashing into the windscreen slightly above his face. He shoved forward on the control column, causing the nose of the chopper to drop so there would be no chance of the pilot's fire ricocheting across the field. Oz then took careful aim and thumbed the firing button for the twin 7.62mm machine guns mounted in the pod to his right.

The bullets from Oz's short burst kicked a cloud of broken concrete to the right of the terrorist. The angry hijacker stopped firing for a moment as Oz backed off slightly and leveled his aircraft.

The hijacker screamed something that was lost in the hurricane of the helicopter's down draft, then lifted his gun and aimed carefully at the American MH-60K.

Oz nosed his chopper forward and thumbed the firing button on the control column, pushing slightly on the left rudder pedal. The chopper's guns spit bullets, the movement of the aircraft fanning the spray of machine-gun fire across the terrorist's chest.

The hijacker jerked spasmodically in the landing light, his weapon creating a stream of fire in the darkness as his finger twitched against the trigger. The submachine gun's magazine was exhausted as the man crumpled to the tarmac, the empty brass from his weapon rolling on the pavement beside him.

"We're clear in here," Victor radioed a moment

later. "The hostages are being checked to be sure we don't have any changelings."

Oz made a tight circle of the 727. "We got the hijacker that escaped," he said. "Take your time checking everyone's ID. You'll have to sit tight for a while so we can get an ordnance team in to clear any booby traps. I can see several wires strung forward and aft of the plane."

"Will do."

Oz flipped to the traffic controller's frequency to request backup from the SAS bomb squad standing by.

3

There was little doubt in Dr. Donald Scharf's mind that the continent of Antarctica was the coldest, most desolate region on earth. He was sick of the barren rocks, the snow, and the ice.

A geologist from UCLA, Dr. Scharf was in Antarctica collecting granite samples and studying plate tectonics. The constant howling of the winds made him nervous; the last few nights he had dreamed of hot baths and a Thanksgiving feast. His black hair itched and was—by his reckoning—nearly a month overdue for a shampoo.

Dr. Scharf brushed the thick lichens off the chunk of granite he'd chipped from an outcropping and dropped the sample into the pouch he carried outside his heavy Cordura-covered parka.

For the umpteenth day in a row, he thought, we're collecting samples from the Neptune Mountain range. The name of the range made Dr. Scharf smirk; it probably did Neptune a disservice. The fossil record might show that the continent had once been a warm land covered with plants and trees, but as Scharf studied the snow-filled valley below, he found it hard to believe that it had ever been anything other than a frosty waste-land.

Dr. Peter Mikhalsky stopped beside Scharf. Mik-halsky was a bear of a man whose fur coat gave him the appearance of a prehistoric animal. Only his face, which was red and deeply lined from extensive periods spent outdoors in the Siberian snow and wind, betrayed his humanity. His gray beard was cut short but still had bits of ice forming in it from his breath.

Scharf eyed the Russian scientist with disdain. Mik-halsky was from Leningrad's Institute of Geology and was tagging along with the UCLA team as a goodwill gesture rather than for any scientific purpose, as far as Scharf was concerned. If it had been the American's de-cision, the Russian would never have come on the expe-dition.

"Today is warm—by Siberian standard," Mikhal-sky said in broken English. He laughed at his joke with a loud bark that irritated Scharf.

"Well, I can't get used to feeling this cold in sum-mer," Dr. Grace Garrett interjected, approaching from behind the two men. "Or having summer in December either, for that matter," she added. Like Scharf, the fe-male geologist was from the University of California at Los Angeles.

Dr. Garrett was dressed in a heavy white parka and wore thick-soled "moon boots" to protect her from the below-freezing temperatures. Her birdlike face was wreathed in short brown hair. Thin-boned and grace-ful, she was often moody. She'd been designated the leader of the group, a position she took seriously. Today she was all business. "Is everyone ready to go?"

"I'm ready," Dr. Harold Cooper said with a tight-lipped smile that kept his teeth from chattering. He blinked behind his thick spectacles, as if in a daze. "I'm not going to find any meteorites here. I don't know how you three talked me into leaving our camp." Cooper was the only astrophysicist in the group.

"Meteorites are the poor man's space probes," he had explained to the team when they'd first met. "The chunks of rock provide us with essential information about the evolution of our solar system. In fact, the bits of stone that are scattered across the Antarctic ice might very well be chunks of the moon or even Mars, kicked up by a meteorite strike millions of years ago." But Cooper knew he wasn't going to find any meteorites on the rocky mountainside and he was ready to leave.

Mikhalsky started down the slope.

"Let's head back down," Dr. Garrett ordered as if the Russian hadn't already started.

Scharf stood still and smirked to himself at Dr. Garrett's attempt to act as if she were their leader. Garrett ignored Scharf, hoisting her heavy bag of samples over her shoulder as if it were a large handbag.

"What we have here?" Dr. Mikhalsky asked as he stopped among the rocks, downhill from the other members of the expedition. His voice was barely audible above the wind whipping across the ridge.

Scharf decided that Mikhalsky had the demeanor of a large animal digging its lair as he pawed with his fur mittens in the rock and snow.

As Mikhalsky continued to labor, Cooper and Garrett started down the slope toward the Russian, creating a minuscule landslide of pebbles that clattered alongside them as they went.

As Scharf neared the group, he saw that the Russian was pulling a large chunk of greenish gray material from the snow.

"What do you make of that?" Mikhalsky asked, holding the fabric in his mittened hands.

"Silk or maybe plastic," Dr. Garrett replied. "But how did it get here?"

"Look there." Cooper pointed, then dropped to his knees and started digging in the ice with his snow ax. In a moment he had uncovered a tin container. As he pulled it from the ice; he discovered it was attached to the fabric by a long silken cord. "I wonder what's in here." He gave it a shake.

"Be careful," Garrett warned him, her voice sounding higher than normal. "We don't know what this thing is."

"Sure we do," Cooper said, searching for an opening to the container. "It's an old weather balloon. Real old, judging from the materials. The balloon looks like a natural fabric, not a synthetic."

"Silk maybe," Mikhalsky suggested.

"Let's take it back to camp," Scharf said. "I'm freezing." He stomped his booted feet against the snow in an effort to increase his circulation.

"How you be cold in all that clothing?" Mikhalsky laughed, glancing at him for a moment. "You Californians too soft."

Scharf said nothing, irritated by the Russian's teasing.

"Let's do take it back to the camp where we can take our time and open it properly," Garrett said, pulling her hood tight. "Soft Californian or not, I'm freezing."

"That okay by myself if we go back to camp to rupture it," Mikhalsky said. "But you have to convince Cooper to wait to unwrap his Christmas present." The Russian broke the momentary silence with another deep laugh while Cooper blinked and adjusted his thick glasses with a mittened hand.

"Uh, sure," Cooper said, smiling. "Christmas present, huh," he added, finally getting the Russian's joke. "Yeah. I'll need my tools to open this." He replaced his ice ax in his belt and helped Mikhalsky fold the silken fabric into a manageable ball that could be carried down the rugged mountainside.

"Let's get going then," Garrett said. She checked to be sure Mt. Hawkes was at their backs, then started down the slope toward the Foundation Ice Stream, the huge glacier on which they'd pitched their tent.

Cooper and Mikhalsky climbed behind her, each carrying one end of the balloon and its deadly tin container that they were planning on opening.

Instead of giving the balloon they'd found a detailed inspection at their base camp, Dr. Peter Mikhalsky and Dr. Harold Cooper had finally bagged it, labeled the artifact, and stored it on the sled along with their rock samples and equipment. The sled was dragged behind their ice tractor two days later when the team returned to Anderson Station.

Anderson Station was located on the Ronne Ice Shelf, four kilometers northeast of the ice-locked Berkner Island, near Gould Bay. It had been established in 1989 and expanded during the Antarctic summer of 1990. Its center was a large geodesic dome that served as the main operations building; within the structure were conference rooms, a canteen, radio communications center, and a recreational room containing a compact library of books, relatively new magazines, and video cassettes.

The large central dome was connected by a series of ice tunnels that radiated outward to eight modest, snow-covered domes and three metal sheds. The central domes and buildings were encompassed by ten storage rooms that had been carved into the snow and connected to it by a rabbit warren of tunnels. The icy passageways made it possible to travel throughout the complex without venturing outdoors.

The smaller domes served a variety of needs and were utilized as laboratories, research centers, and living quarters for the forty-one scientists, engineers, and military personnel who manned Anderson Station. One of the secondary domes in the station was conspicuous by its distance from the others; this held a nuclear reactor that generated power and heat for the station.

The Anderson Station complex was part of the United States Antarctic Research Program and was administered by the National Science Foundation, which gave grants and contracted US scientists to do various types of research in Antarctica. The station was supported by commercial contractors on occasion, though the bulk of supplies was brought in by the US Navy, US Air Force, and US Coast Guard.

The major resupply of the station occurred each year during the frigid summer of the continent. During the winter, when darkness prevailed during the long nights, much of the Antarctic Ocean would become frozen into what was called the "ice pack." Howling winds and temperatures dipping to ninety degrees below zero Fahrenheit would cause the ice pack to grow continuously until it stretched from the coast for hundreds of miles into the ocean.

In October, spring brought its warming trend. The ice pack would then break apart with spring's sunlight, high winds, and warmer weather. Then huge, flat-topped icebergs five hundred to a thousand feet tall would break from the edge of the icy sheet covering the area and float beyond the ice pack. When summer approached, icebreakers could again crash through the ice floe to reach the shore. This path cut through the ice would allow supply ships to bring stocks to the scientists based at Anderson Station.

During the long Antarctic winter, the station could be supplied only at great expense, mostly by stocks flown in on helicopters. Unlike larger stations, Anderson had no runway that could accommodate fixed-wing planes. And even if it had, keeping the runway cleared of the drifting snow and ice would have been impossible, given the limited manpower. Therefore, the station had to store enough food and other supplies to be self-sufficient from one visit by the icebreaker and the supply ships following it to the next.

Three days after their return to Anderson Station, Dr. Cooper found time to help Dr. Mikhalsky in "dissecting the balloon," as the Russian put it. The two had secured permission to utilize the animal research laboratory for their impromptu investigation since the lab was not yet manned.

The two scientists walked through an ice tunnel toward the animal research laboratory's dome. Both wore heavy coats; their breath formed clouds of mist in the frosty air when they exhaled. Dr. Mikhalsky carried a heavy plastic bag containing the balloon they'd found days earlier. Dr. Cooper held a green nylon tool bag containing the instruments he often used to inspect and collect meteorites.

"So let's hope it isn't like old joke," Mikhalsky said. He glanced toward Cooper and was pleased to see a confused blinking from behind the American's spectacles. "You know. We work and work to open tin on balloon and inside it say, 'Kilroy was here.'"

Cooper chuckled. "Or maybe it'll be a tiny bit more up-to-date and say 'Eat at Joe's.' That's what they always had in the cartoons in the fifties."

" 'Eat at Joe's'?" Mikhalsky asked, frowning because it was his turn to be puzzled.

"Yeah. An advertisement for a restaurant named Joe's."

"Ah. Like billboard?"

"Right. Here we are."

The two stopped in front of a heavy steel door. Cooper fished a scrap of paper with the door's combination scribbled on it from his coat pocket. His breath formed frost on the door as he bent to tap the correct code into the numerical key lock. "I don't understand why they lock everything at this place. It's not like we're in a high crime area or someone's going to wander in off the glacier."

"Perhaps they worry about having Russian around."

"I hope you're joking. That doesn't sound too good for East/West relations." Cooper swung the door aside and entered the darkened dome that was lit only by a series of skylights.

"No. It's true. Russians notorious pack rats." He followed Cooper into the dome. "Supplies so scarce in past that we liberate anything not fastened down. If you own car in Moscow, you have keep windshield wipers in trunk, or someone steal them. Tanks don't run half time because troops strip parts from comrades' tanks and hide them for *their* tanks when break down."

"I think I'm beginning to understand why they lock the doors here," Cooper said with a laugh. He flipped on a bank of switches and the fluorescent lights above them flickered to life.

The domed lab was forty feet across with small storage rooms, closets, and a restroom branching from it. Fire extinguishers were positioned along the walls. The shelves, tables, and desks that filled the white plastic and steel laboratory were empty, as were the various-sized animal cages and aquariums.

"Here?" Mikhalsky pointed to a large stainless steel table that lay under a brightly lit area of the ceiling.

"Looks good." Cooper followed Mikhalsky's example and removed his coat and draped it over a metal chair. He checked the thermostat on the wall to be sure the electrical heaters in the dome were set properly.

Within five minutes the two scientists had the old balloon unpacked and draped across the table. After inspecting the silken fabric and finding no markings on the exterior of the material, they removed the dented tin tied to it. This they carried to a second empty table. Cooper snapped on the floodlight overhead so the container was bathed in light.

The scratched tin was oddly shaped. It consisted of a cube that was soldered onto a large canlike upper section. A ring atop the whole assembly had secured it to the balloon.

Cooper extracted a diamond-toothed hacksaw from his tool bag. He carefully removed the blade and replaced it with a similar one with fine teeth.

"I don't have a clue which section might contain sensitive instruments," Cooper said. "Any such devices would undoubtedly have been shattered by the travel of the balloon across the rocks, anyway. Those dents and scratches didn't get there by gentle treatment." Cooper turned the cube over. "I'll start here. It looks like there's a soldered seam. It might break open once we get it started."

The American stroked the surface of the tin a few times to get a rough spot that the saw teeth could cut into. He worked slowly, taking care not to overheat the blade and damage it or overcut the metal and mar the contents of the tin.

"There," Cooper finally announced after cutting a narrow hole in the metal surface. He reached into his tool bag and retrieved a slender steel and plastic probe. "Now . . . If I can pry it open."

He levered the tool in the slit. The tin bent inward and then suddenly split along one of its seams exposing a complicated mechanism of gears and springs. Cooper poked it a couple of times with the probe.

"Look like old alarm clock," Mikhalsky ventured.

"Or a time bomb," Cooper said.

The Russian swore in his native tongue.

"Don't worry," the American reassured him. "It looks like most of the chemical that was in that container has eaten into the metal and neutralized itself. And those gears are so corroded they can't move."

"Wait minute. Look there." Mikhalsky pointed to a lilliputian decal inside the tin wall of the device.

"Hmmm," Cooper muttered, then rummaged through his tool case again. He extracted a leather pouch that he unsnapped to remove a large magnifying glass. "Let's see what that is. Hopefully it's not 'Kilroy was here.' "

The Russian stepped back and looked over Cooper's shoulder as the American focused the magnifying glass on the decal. The tiny rectangle had a red sun on a white background.

"Japanese flag, isn't it?" Cooper asked.

"Yes. Most certainly."

"Must have come from one of the Japanese bases. But that'd make it only a few years old, I'd think. Most of their camps haven't been here for that long."

"That's not flag they fly today," Mikhalsky remarked softly. "That's imperial flag of Japanese Empire. Balloon must be World War II vintage."

"That's weird. How in the world would it have gotten here? They didn't have any stations in the Antarctic then, did they?"

"Let's see what is in top," Mikhalsky suggested. "Perhaps we learn more if we see what is there."

"Okay. This seam runs into that section. I'll use the probe to jimmy it some more . . ."

Cooper levered the tool and the case suddenly split open. A cloud of brown dust rose as spores erupted from the tin, covering the surface of the table and the two scientists.

"What hell is that?" Mikhalsky asked, trying to clap the material off his hands and brush it from his sleeves.

"Come on," Cooper sputtered, spitting out the dust that had gotten into his mouth. "The emergency showers are over here. There's no telling what this stuff might be."

The two men quickly jumped into the showers without removing their clothing and washed in the water. After shaking a small amount of the dustlike spores from their coats and collecting a sample in a small glass vial, they donned their jackets over their wet clothing and left the lab.

After hearing the two men's story, the station commander ordered the laboratory left sealed until opened by the National Science Council scientists who would occupy the lab the next summer. With that, the commander dismissed the two soggy scientists, admonishing them to get dry before they froze into blocks of ice.

Cooper and Mikhalsky, soaked and contrite, resumed their normal duties. Two days later, a UH-IN helicopter dropped off a small load of supplies and mail. The package containing the vial of dust from the balloon was placed on the helicopter, starting its long trip to the United States.

Four hours after the helicopter departed, Cooper developed a severe headache and reported to the base's doctor.

5

Oz stood watching the three Army work crews disassemble and prepare each of the three MH-60K helicopters for transportation to Fort Bragg. Although his people and the members of the Delta Team had finished their rescue efforts in Sydney, their work with the mission was far from concluded; they still faced a long trip home and the debriefing session that always followed an operation.

Oz was so keyed up on adrenaline following the rescue, he paced around the hangar like a caged animal. He ate a sandwich from an airport vending machine and tried to calm down.

Sergeant Bruce Marvin supervised the loading team that would spend their next hour preparing Oz's helicopter for the transport plane. The neckless, bulldog-headed man motioned with arms muscled from a decade of sweating and straining while he repaired, disassembled, or reassembled Army helicopters. "All right," Marvin said to his crew, and then paused.

" 'You know the drill,' " his men finished, the words permanently etched in their minds.

The sergeant managed to hide the beginnings of

a smile with a gruff frown. "Let's get with it then. Clean her inside and out."

The helicopter was rapidly cleaned and partially disassembled for shipment. Designed for air transport, the MH-60K had rotors and tail fins that folded into a compact load that could be squeezed into the cargo plane's rear hatch. The chopper's rotor was lowered and the hydraulic pressure in its landing gear decreased to give the machine a squat profile so it would fit in the transport plane. Finally, a loading manifest was assembled by Marvin's team and components that had been removed from the helicopters inventoried. After the crew had added tiedown plates and fittings to the helicopter, they guided it into its preload position behind the transport along with the other two helicopters that had gone through identical preparations.

In short order the crews had the three helicopters loaded and secured on the Lockheed C-5A "Galaxy" cargo plane. The entire job of preparing and loading the helicopters required slightly less than two hours. Once this task was accomplished, Oz and his flight team, the ground crews, and the Delta Team climbed aboard the huge, swept-winged transport that would take them to the States.

The C-5A cargo plane was almost sixty-eight meters wide and over seventy-five meters long; it rested on its twenty-eight-wheel landing system, close to the runway. Its rear cargo hatch had been lowered to form a ramp that permitted the men and machines to enter the plane. From its camouflaged wings hung four powerful turbofan jet engines.

The MH-60Ks were stored on the lower deck of the transport. The Night Stalker personnel and Delta troops rode in the pressurized and air-conditioned upper deck. Most of the men catnapped in their sweat-stained clothes or talked softly during the first leg of their journey.

Oz found himself thinking about the evening before the mission had begun. He'd been standing backstage at the Fayetteville Civic Auditorium, feeling awkward and out of place among the civilians surrounding him, who wore expensive suits and gowns.

"Here he is," Jessica Rose had said, taking Oz by the arm. "Dr. Wahl, this is Captain Jefferson Davis Carson—known to his friends as Oz."

"Ah, you're the talented young man who made Jessica's lute," the bushy-eyebrowed conductor said as he squeezed Oz's hand. "I've heard lutes and violins made by Stradivarius and I swear their tones aren't any sweeter than those made by your lute. You must tell me how you achieve this sound."

"That's Oz's secret," Jessica said, laughing, still holding the pilot's arm. She gave him a sideward glance with her long-lashed brown eyes.

Oz was suddenly conscious of just how young the college senior looked. And how fetching she was in her low-cut formal.

"Oz's father was a chemist," she continued. "I think he developed the varnish." Jessica smiled, again displaying her even teeth. "And it has something to do with the bracing inside, but that's all I can extract from him."

"It's one fantastic instrument," Dr. Wahl asserted.

"Jessica is the one who deserves the credit," Oz said, turning to the young woman and trying to change the subject. "Your solo work in the Vivaldi concerto was outstanding, Jessica, and I've never seen a standing ovation like the one you received."

"Neither have I," Dr. Wahl agreed, his brows nearly meeting. "I hope you're coming to our party," he said to Oz.

"Well . . ."

"Yes, you said you would," Jessica insisted.

"You should give us a chance to ply you with alcohol so we can get the secret of your varnish," the conductor said, only half in jest.

Oz's beeper sounded, saving him from having to commit himself. He pulled it from his pocket, smiling sheepishly at Jessica and muttering an apology. He found a pay phone backstage and dialed the number of the base. He was given a coded message that told him hostages had been taken and his services as a pilot were needed immediately.

Oz had made an excuse, and Jessica had clearly been crestfallen. Now he rode in the dark cargo plane, unsure what his emotions had been when he'd been forced to leave. Part of him had wanted to stay and sweep the pretty lutist off her feet. Part of him had been relieved—he'd felt guilty when she'd held his arm, even though Sandy's lawyers had served him with divorce papers that were now finalized. Jessica's too young anyway, he thought, leaning back and trying to sleep as the jet engines droned.

The cargo plane's six-hour hop ended at American Samoa where they refueled and then flew on to Honolulu. Here the flight was laid over at Wheeler Air Force Base so Oz and the others involved in the action could be debriefed by US Army Intelligence.

After landing, Oz and his crew found themselves

trudging along a palm-lined sidewalk toward a single-story whitewashed building where the military intelligence officers and Captain Louis Warner, the division commander of the Night Stalkers, waited for them.

Oz glanced upward at the nearly cloudless sky. The hot Hawaiian sun bore down on them and made it seem as if they were still in Australia.

"I hate debriefings," O.T. muttered, wiping beads of sweat from his smooth-shaven head with the palm of his hand.

"They're necessary, though," Luger said.

"Out of the mouths of babes," O.T. said, laughing. "I know debriefings help us keep from making mistakes in the future, but they're a pain in the butt just the same."

They walked up the front steps of the building and Oz shoved his way through the glass and steel front door. The pilot presented his green military ID to the duty officer and was waved down the hallway.

That night Oz slept the dreamless sleep of a man who has been pushed to near collapse. He awoke in the morning, wolfed down a huge plate of steak and eggs, and was soon on the C-5A with his comrades headed for the US mainland. The plane made a refueling stop in Los Angeles, then headed south to complete the mission assigned them before they had been diverted to Australia.

Once they were again in the air aboard a C-5A transport, Oz briefed the leaders of the three Night Stalker crews and Lieutenant James Victor, who commanded the platoon of Delta Force troops accompanying them.

"As you know," Oz told them over the drone of

the jet engines, "after our refueling stops, we'll reach McTavish Station. That's in West Antarctica near Newman Glacier, northeast of Mt. Ulmer." He pointed to a map O.T. and Luger had spread between them. "McTavish is a small base that's open only during the Antarctic summer—and it's summer there now, though you won't be able to tell. It does have a runway large enough to accommodate a C-5A."

"No chance for sunbathing?" Victor asked with a poker face.

"Not unless you're a penguin," Oz answered. "Instead of sunbathing, we'll engage in a series of exercises at McTavish. These will be designed to give us a number of new capabilities—including the ability to operate in extreme cold and on the open seas. Concurrently with the cold-weather exercises, we'll also be testing out the experimental CONCOP helicopter and engaging in naval operations.

"We'll carry these two exercises out with two Night Stalker teams at a time, one team in the CONCOP and the other with the Navy. Death Song and I will take the CONCOP first."

"Isn't the CONCOP the chopper that's being called the 'Suicide Machine' by the press?" one of the other Night Stalker pilots asked.

"Right," Oz answered. "The CONCOP's had problems in the past, but they're supposed to be cleaned up. But if any of us run into any troubles with the CONCOP, we'll scratch this portion of the exercise.

"As to the naval exercises, one team at a time will fly over the glacier out to the Weddell Sea where they'll work with two Navy destroyers, the *Patrick Henry* and the *Thomas Jefferson.* These ships normally carry one

Seahawk helicopter, but the *Patrick Henry* will have its helicopter stowed so we can use its landing deck.

"Once on board, we'll then have the new modular version of the Seahawk's sonobuoy dispenser, a dipping sonar, and two torpedoes mounted on our choppers. This will enable us to carry out submarine-hunting exercises with the Seahawk from the *Thomas Jefferson*. As I understand it, they'll furnish the personnel to run the sonar on our helicopters."

"But we'll get to control the torpedoes?" Death Song asked.

"Right," Oz answered with a grin. "They're saving the real goodies for our navigators to run."

Oz continued: "I can't stress enough the need for extreme care during both phases of our exercise. The excessive cold and the experimental nature of CON-COP and the equipment at sea add a lot of variables we're not used to. Things could become dangerous in a hurry. I don't want any chopper jocking and no heroics. Just do your job and don't daydream.

"Any questions?" Oz paused and studied the faces of those around him. "Okay, then. You may brief your men."

Lieutenant Victor and the three helicopter pilots stood and walked briskly down the aisles of the C-5A to where their men and crews were sitting in the web-backed seats.

"You guys have any questions?" Oz asked his own crew.

No one spoke.

"Then I'm going to take a nap," Oz told them. "It's going to be a long two weeks. You're all free to go wherever you want—as long as you don't get out of your seats."

"Thanks," Luger said with a grin.

"We won't be out too late, Dad," O.T. cracked.

The C-5A landed without incident on the runway carved from the ice at McTavish Station. The cargo hatch opened slowly on its hydraulic arms and a freezing wind whipped through the plane, instantly chilling everyone inside.

Death Song pulled his parka hood around his face as he plodded in his white "Mickey Mouse" boots toward the open rear door of the C-5A. "It's sure not Hawaii," he groused.

"I'm glad it's not hot," Luger offered as he disembarked. "I hate being hot all the time. I don't know how people stand living in those island paradises."

Oz paused to slap Sergeant Bruce Marvin on the shoulder. "Certainly don't envy the ground crew today, Sergeant Marvin."

"Sometimes you do envy us, sir?" Marvin replied in his traditional gruff manner.

"Well," Oz said, laughing, "unloading helicopters in this weather is going to be worse than usual. Good luck."

"Thank you, sir."

Oz left the ramp at the rear of the cargo plane, putting on his Gargoyle sunglasses to protect his eyes from the bright Antarctic sunlight and the stinging ice blown by the wind. He studied the bleak landscape.

McTavish Station was not very impressive, Oz thought. The central buildings were surrounded by colored flags that dotted the snow, each marking positions where pipes and cables ran under the ice. The flags snapped in the sharp wind.

A large geodesic dome of aluminum and plastic formed most of the complex. Three large metal sheds stood in squared-off contrast to the curved dome west of them. A second petite dome that looked like a giant golf ball was to the south; it contained the nuclear reactor supplying power to the complex.

Oz watched a snow tractor sputtering away from the station. It pulled a sled piled high with supplies for a scientific expedition that was departing toward the peaks in the distance. Three skiers dressed in red and yellow snowsuits were hitching a ride, holding on to the sled.

Two other men dressed in parkas trudged toward the C-5A. "Captain Carson?" queried the one in the blue parka as he approached Oz.

"Yes," Oz answered.

"My name's Bill Howard." The speaker made no effort to shake hands since both he and Oz wore heavy mittens. "I'll take you and your men to what we generously call our canteen. Give you a chance to stretch your legs and see that there really is food that's worse than the Army's."

Bill Howard took the Night Stalker and Delta teams to the small dome containing the station's canteen. Oz was pleasantly surprised to find that the meal of roast beef, potatoes, and carrots was quite good; the servings were huge.

Oz remarked on the size of the meal to one of the men standing in line at the canteen.

"You'll discover you burn off a lot more energy in the cold," he explained to Oz. "Just walking around outside in the heavy clothing burns off a lot of calories. That's not to mention the energy it takes to keep warm."

After killing an hour talking to the station's commander, Oz received word that the CONCOP was fueled and ready. He located Death Song and they carefully suited up in their heavy cold-weather gear and prepared to take the small helicopter on its first exercise.

Oz felt sweat forming on his hands and underarms, despite the cold wind blowing across the icy plain. Nerves, he mused, squinting at the bright, cloudless sky. He was worried about flying the CONCOP. Even though he'd spent hours in the simulator, he knew the real thing would be different—and dangerous. Despite a careful battery of testing, four of the other prototypes had crashed; the accidents were as yet unexplained.

The Reed-Dallas CONCOP was an impressive machine. It was barely fifteen meters long but carried more armament than many larger helicopters. Its stark, black surface made it look like a hole in the snow surrounding it. Its rotors were mounted high and toward the front of the helicopter, which allowed them to be tilted far forward for a maximum speed and range nearly a quarter greater than most larger helicopters.

The CONCOP had been designed for quick alteration from one operational configuration to another. Stripped, the chopper could function as a scout helicopter. Configured as it presently was, the CONCOP had been described by one military journal as a "twenty-first-century, rotary wing fighter-jock."

Oz and Death Song opened the cockpit and climbed inside. Death Song sat in the gunner/navigator seat in the nose of the CONCOP while Oz rode at the rear of the dual cockpit.

The instruments in front of Oz were organized almost identically to those in the MH-60K he normally flew. The chopper was more automated, however, and featured a heads-up display, or HUD, similar to that found in many jet fighters and a computer system that "talked" during critical operations. Oz noticed the new-plastic smell of the machine.

Death Song carefully latched the canopy over his head. In a short time he had the navigational and weapons systems operational. He tested the aiming system that was coupled to the 5.56mm Minigun in the turret below the helicopter. When he looked at something outside the helicopter, infrared beams and detectors mounted on his helmet and in the cockpit fed into the aircraft's computer and servo-motor system causing the Minigun as well as a forward-looking infrared camera to mimic his head movements.

The Minigun and FLIR camera were slaved together and functioned as if they were part of the gunner's body, with the picture being displayed in a small screen over his right eye. This gave him the ability to "see" into the heat or infrared region with his right eye while viewing things as they normally appeared with his left. The FLIR thermal-imaging device made it possible to detect warm objects that were often otherwise hidden during the day or night.

A belt of four thousand 5.56mm cartridges fed into the Minigun's four barrels, giving it the ability to riddle any soft targets Death Song might choose to attack; the turret that contained the gun was designed to collapse harmlessly upward if the helicopter crashed on its belly.

To deal with armored targets, the CONCOP had two hardpoints on its stubby pylons, one on each side of the fuselage. On the right pylon was a pod containing twenty-four ballistic 2.75-inch rockets similar to those on the MH-60K helicopters. On the left pylon were four Hellfire missiles that could be guided to target with a laser designator located in the FLIR assembly.

Most of the navigational display was nearly identical to that of the MH-60K. It included an integrated system with a Doppler inertial navigation system, dual mission computers, and a multiplexer data bus. The information from this equipment was displayed on a dual green phosphor CRT "TV" in front of the pilot and navigator. The screens had prompt keys along their sides to allow accessing information from different sources within the chopper. Because of the integration of the cathode ray tube displays, only seventeen instrument gauges were to be found on the console. In addition to being available from the console, many of the instrument readouts were available in the form of an HUD.

"How's it look?" Oz asked over the intercom.

"All systems are operational," Death Song said, checking the console in front of him. "We're ready to fly."

After calling for permission for takeoff, Oz revved

the engine and pulled the collective pitch lever, instantly aware of how differently the CONCOP handled.

Within moments the helicopter had climbed to six hundred feet and was shooting over the low range of ice hills east of McTavish. Oz guided the chopper above the slope and down the other side in a giddy fall that took them toward the icy valley on the other side of the peaks.

"Any sign of problems?" Death Song asked.

"No," Oz replied. He studied the helicopter's instrument display in front of him. "But the controls just don't feel right, somehow. I can't quite put my finger on it . . . I don't know, maybe it's just the fly-by-wire system." He paused a moment. "I'm taking us east and higher over the next range of hills. That will bring us to the range, won't it?"

Death Song studied his instruments and punched up coordinates. "Yeah. Here you go," he said as a map of the area appeared on the display in front of Oz.

The pilot watched the map as he kicked the right rudder pedal to bring the helicopter around and locked it onto course. As they swooped over the hills, Oz said, "That has to be it below us."

An acre-wide plain of rusted barrels, trash, and discarded vehicles, the leftovers from an Italian base that had been abandoned years before, was sprawled below them.

"What an eyesore," Death Song observed as they circled the junk-covered field. "No wonder they don't mind if we practice with our weapons here. It's a shame they didn't clean this up before they abandoned it."

"Yeah," Oz agreed. "Maybe we'll help a little bit

by pounding some of this stuff to bits. Arm the weapons."

"Master arm," Death Song announced. He ran his hands across the buttons controlling the chopper's armament.

"You retain control of the rockets and gun," Oz directed the navigator. "I want to concentrate on flying. I'm still not satisfied with how it's handling."

Death Song adjusted the control settings for the weapons. "Okay. I've got 'em."

Oz craned his neck, searching the air for other aircraft. "Looks clear here. Do you see anything?"

"Negative. And no sign of any other aircraft on our radar."

"All right. I'll make a quick pass over the field if you want to try your Minigun." Oz brought the helicopter around, gaining speed as he dropped toward the junkyard. A ripping sound came from under his feet as Death Song fired short bursts from the Minigun. The brief eruptions of fire pocked and chewed the metal cans and barrels under the chopper.

"This is great," Death Song exulted. "Looks *can* kill in this baby."

Oz circled the junkyard, the shadow of the CONCOP flickering in the snow below. Then he took the chopper for a low rushing pass of the dump. Again Death Song peppered the refuse with machine-gun fire as Oz zigzagged the chopper over the field.

"Let's try the Hellfires," Death Song suggested after they'd completed their run.

"Let me get some altitude," Oz said. Even though the Hellfires mounted on the CONCOP pylon had dummy warheads, Oz wanted to make the run as realistic as possible. He brought up the collective pitch lever and the tiny helicopter soared into the air.

In the front of the helicopter's cockpit, Death Song activated the target acquisition and designation sight. The TADS would guide a missile to any target the system indicated when the gunner simply looked at it and activated the laser.

Oz briskly accelerated to one thousand feet, leveled out, and rushed through a steep turn to position the CONCOP for a missile strike. The helicopter seemed to hang in space for a second; then it started a near free-fall descent toward the plain far below.

Abruptly the control column shivered in his hand and a warning light started flashing.

"Warning," the computer alarm spoke in the cockpit. "You are exceeding the flight speed of the helicopter. Warning: you are—"

Oz snapped the mechanical voice off. "We're hardly moving," Oz said as he stopped the descent of the helicopter by raising the collective pitch lever. "That's a bug they'll have to remove from the system. You ready for the missile launch?"

"All ready," Death Song replied.

"Here we go." Oz depressed the collective pitch lever and eased forward on the control column, starting their fall toward the junkyard far below. As Oz held the control column tightly in his right hand, it shuddered again and suddenly went limp.

The CONCOP continued its slow dive.

"My control column's dead back here," Oz called to Death Song. "So's the collective pitch lever. Try yours."

Death Song quickly grasped the column and

pulled back in an effort to halt their fall. They continued downward, their speed increasing as they descended toward the ice far below. "I have no response from either," the navigator warned.

Oz frantically tried the column again. It shifted unresponsively. "Radio McTavish and let them know what's happening. I'm going to cut the power to the engine and see if we can gyrocoast down."

"Will do," Death Song replied.

The engine wound down immediately. This should have locked the rotors into their optimum position to allow them to brake the fall; instead, there was actually an increase in the rate of the helicopter's descent.

This is what caused the other crashes, Oz thought. But he found little comfort in this knowledge, since he was about to suffer the same fate.

None of the pilots avoided a crash by SOP, Oz told himself. Going by the book wasn't going to save the chopper. He decided to depart from standard operating procedures and try something else. He had nothing to lose; the ground was racing toward them.

Oz throttled the engine back to life. He felt the control column become rigid, then go limp again as the engine sputtered. "Almost," he said aloud. He shut off the engine and tried the procedure again.

This time the control column came to life. Oz carefully pulled it back and raised the collective pitch lever. Their rate of descent decreased slightly but the ground continued to rush toward them.

Oz lifted the collective pitch lever higher. The machine's engine and rotors strained to stop their plunge. Little by little their rate of fall decreased until finally they were hovering, just forty feet over the ice, when their free-fall finally leveled off.

"Real close!" Death Song said, exploding a burst of air. "What the hell happened?"

Oz exhaled deeply. "That's one for the engineers. But I'm willing to bet the computer has a glitch in its program that disconnects the controls from the system."

"No wonder they've had trouble with the CON-COPs," Death Song exclaimed. "Thanks for getting us out of that!"

"Don't be too grateful. I was more worried about my hide than yours. Now let's see if we can get this hi-tech death trap back in and make a report."

"So those are the fish we'll be using to hunt ships?"
O.T. pointed toward the torpedoes on the side of the
helicopter's pylon. "I wonder how far the military will
go? Any bets that they'll have us carrying an ICBM before long?"

"Or maybe an X-ray laser," Luger suggested.

"Well, all kidding aside," Death Song said in a
hushed voice, "I overheard Lieutenant Warner talking
about a particle-beam weapon for both the door gunners."

"Okay, junior bird men, let's climb aboard," Oz
ordered without a smile.

The four crewmen mounted the helicopter, kicking the snow off their boots as they entered. Death Song
and Oz buckled themselves in and initiated their preflight check of the instruments.

O.T. and Luger adjusted the GE M134 Miniguns
that normally poked their six-barreled muzzles from the
gunners' doors on either side of the aircraft and then
stowed them inside their compartments. The Gatling-
like weapons were fed from four-thousand-round
linked belts and powered by electric motors that en-

abled them to shoot two to four thousand rounds per minute. The weapons were suitable for engaging unarmored aircraft, ground vehicles, or troops. The spade-gripped weapons had a large twin-ring rear sight and a ten-round burst control that could be engaged to conserve on ammunition when necessary.

O.T. checked the two flexible chutes, pointing out the door, that expelled brass and links from empty cartridges. Satisfied that everything was as it should be, he plugged the cord from his helmet into the chopper's intercom system and buckled himself into the seat beside his Minigun.

Moments later Oz lifted the chopper into the frigid air. He was instantly aware of how different the machine felt with the two torpedoes aboard. He rotated the nose of the MH-60K eastward and eased the control column slowly forward, gradually acquiring more speed as he got a feel for the new configuration.

"How's she feel?" Death Song asked.

"Awkward," Oz admitted. "Like we're carrying two torpedoes on the port side. I'll let you fly it in a few minutes and you'll see what I mean. Overall it's pretty much like the simulator—a little sluggish in turns and slightly slower to react. We're going to have to be careful until we get the hang of it."

Oz wheeled the MH-60K around McTavish Station and headed northeast, toward the destroyer waiting for them in the Weddell Sea. He forced himself to relax, even though he continued to be apprehensive about the exercises they faced.

Harold Cooper was convinced the medic at Anderson Station had been mistaken in his diagnosis. The throbbing headache was not what Cooper associated with a common cold. So he returned to the station's medical room.

"My 'two aspirins and call me in the morning' didn't work, huh?" Dr. Mark Sanders joked, noting the odd coloration of Cooper's eyes. The doctor crushed out his cigarette and stood to welcome the patient into his compact office.

"If it's any consolation," the doctor continued, waving Cooper toward the examination table, "at least three fourths of the station is coming down with the bug you have."

"Well," Cooper said, "I feel terrible."

"I'm not surprised you got sick after that soaking shower you had. Mikhalsky seems to have fared better. He just has the sniffles."

"Well, the aspirin didn't help," Cooper sneered, climbing onto the table. "You must be saving the painkillers for yourself."

The doctor was puzzled, then decided the scientist

must be joking. The doctor smiled again. "Let's take a look at your throat. That's it . . ." He stuck a tongue depressor into Cooper's open mouth. "It looks a little inflamed in there." He reached for a scalpel and a cotton swab. "Since you were the first one to contract this bug, I'd like to take a sample for lab tests."

The doctor turned toward Cooper and was taken totally by surprise. Cooper's fist clipped Sanders across the bridge of the nose, making his eyes water in pain. Cooper then kicked the doctor in the groin.

Sanders gasped. The scalpel he'd held clattered across the floor.

"I knew you were going to cut my throat so you could keep the medicine I need!" Cooper said evenly. He yanked the goose-necked lamp off the doctor's desk and swung it.

"What!" The doctor stepped back as the first swing missed him. Cornered against the wall, the doctor was grazed by the second blow. He stumbled under a third and then fell to his knees as another impact caught him in the nose before he could lift his hands to shield his face.

The steel lamp swung again, and again, striking the doctor across the base of the skull. The wounded medic sprawled to the floor amid the broken shards of the light bulb, his body shaking spasmodically.

Cooper commenced to kick savagely with his heavy boots.

Then Cooper stopped. He gazed calmly at the still form at his feet.

"First you keep the painkillers for yourself and then you try to cut my throat with that scalpel," Cooper whispered, an expression of satisfaction on his face.

Now I'll have to hide my crime, Cooper thought. Undoubtedly others at the station were working with the doctor. The damned junkies were everywhere, trying to steal the medications decent people needed. Cooper knew they'd be out to get him as well, especially now that he'd killed their ringleader. He'd have to be careful. He bent over, snatched the scalpel from the floor, and hid it in his pocket.

Screaming that the commander of the base was attempting to kill him, the naval captain in charge of the nuclear generator at Anderson Station took Dr. Grace Garrett hostage, sealed the door to the tunnel leading to the power plant, and initiated the emergency shutdown procedure for the reactor.

The captain pulled her into the room; Dr. Garrett struggled, then stood still as she stared at the dead technician who lay bludgeoned at her feet. The alarm bells continued to clang in the room as the captain pulled another large slide switch. Instantly the electricity to the entire complex was shut down. The lights in the reactor room flickered and then switched to their emergency circuits and battery-powered lights flooded the room in their harsh glare.

Someone was banging at the door to the reactor. Garrett decided it was the only chance for escape and ran for the door—but the captain blocked her exit.

"I know you've been plotting with the commander to kill me," the captain whispered, brandishing a large crescent wrench in front of Dr. Garrett's eyes. "You even planted him to stop me," he said, pointing toward the body lying in the corner.

"I didn't do—" Garrett started.

"But I've got the commander by the short hair, now," the captain muttered, his eyes glazing over. "He'll be pissing icicles before long."

Dr. Garrett backed away from the captain, her eyes wide with fear. Without warning, he leapt forward and slammed the heavy wrench he held across her skull. She crumpled to the floor.

The captain watched her a second and saw no movement. He spun and crossed to the heavy steel door leading into the reactor room and placed his ear to its surface.

On the other side of the door, six members of the naval staff assigned to the station stood in the ice tunnel, now in near darkness except for the dim, bluish sunlight filtering through the ceiling above the tunnel.

"The fool's changed the combination," Ensign Davidson muttered, rubbing at his brow in an effort to suppress the headache that seemed to be cracking his scalp apart. In frustration he suddenly hammered at the numerical lock with his fist.

"There's no way we're going to get through this steel door before the base freezes," Wendel quietly suggested, unconsciously licking his chapped lips. "Let's go outside and see if we can enter through the emergency exit."

"I'll decide what's to be done!" Ensign Davidson yelled, placing his hand on the holstered pistol strapped to his waist.

"Take it easy, sir," Warrant Officer Brown said, raising his mittened hands. "I'm sure Wendel meant nothing . . . It really isn't a bad idea—going outdoors to—"

"You guys don't want me to get into the reactor

room, do you?'' Ensign Davidson asked in a low voice. "You're trying to sabotage the station, too, aren't you?''

The handgun was in his bare hand before anyone could react. He fired as fast as he could pull the trigger. The five men encircling him were downed in a flurry of smoke and bullets.

His pistol empty, Davidson calmly ejected the spent magazine and inserted a new load of ammunition into its base. Two of the men on the ice floor moaned; Wendel struggled to rise. Davidson thumbed the release on his pistol and the slide clattered forward, shoving a cartridge into its chamber.

The ensign methodically put a bullet into the brain of each of the men on the ice floor around him. Unemotionally he inspected the havoc, then spoke in a low voice, "They're not going to take me.''

He placed the firearm's barrel into his mouth and pulled the trigger.

Mikhalsky stood next to the radioman at Anderson Station as the sergeant repeated his frantic message for help as the mob battered down the door.

Dr. Scharf rushed in and stabbed the radioman in the back, then reached out and jerked the microphone from the instrument panel.

"There's the Soviet spy!" Scharf shrieked as Mikhalsky ran from the blood-splattered room and ducked into the second ice tunnel connecting the radio to the rest of the base.

Later, Mikhalsky had hidden in a hallway. The mob Dr. Scharf was leading roamed the dark corridors screaming curses as they demanded Mikhalsky's death.

The Russian tried to forget the scene in the radio room. He cowered in the near darkness of the tunnel.

The people that had been chasing him had started arguing and fighting among themselves. There was a flurry of shouting, then a quiet, deathly calm in the ice tunnels leading from Mikhalsky's hiding place.

Everyone has surely gone mad, the scientist thought. Anderson Station had lost its power; soon it would be frozen solid with no water and no heat. And supplies would be hard to secure, thanks to the inferno in the canteen and food storage rooms, which had been set by a hysterical cook who claimed he'd been skipped for promotion because his grandparents were German.

We're dead men here, the Russian decided. Even if he succeeded in staying hidden from the crazed occupants of the station, he'd freeze or starve.

There was only one possible escape from the madness. If he could elude Scharf and the others long enough to flee to the outdoors, there was a chance he might steal a snow tractor and drive it to the nearby Soviet station.

The probability of failure horrified him: lack of fuel in the tractor, failure to find a route to the other station, or a chance blizzard . . . Any of a hundred variables would spell his imminent death.

Shots rang out in the hall, sending a shower of ice into the air. Mikhalsky jumped to his feet and bounded down the dark corridor.

One thing is sure, the Russian told himself as he again crouched in the darkness. It would be better to take his chances outside in a storm.

Minutes later Mikhalsky broke through a skylight

and climbed out of the ice tunnel he'd been hiding in. The Russian blinked in the snow that swirled over him and then started for the nearest snow tractor, parked near the central dome of the station.

"Patrick Henry," Oz radioed to the destroyer he was approaching. "This is NS-1, requesting permission to land, over."

"NS-1, we're reading you loud and clear. Permission to land is granted. Approach the landing deck from the north. The seas are calm so you won't need to wench yourself down, over."

"Thank you, *Patrick Henry,* over and out."

The *Patrick Henry* had a deceptive appearance. At first glance the gray ship appeared to be armed with only the five-inch cannon sitting in the turret on the foredeck, a red circle painted around it to keep crew hands out of the dangerous radius its barrel might quickly transverse when in operation.

In fact, the 466-foot-long destroyer was armed to the teeth.

On the foredeck behind the cannon sat a Mark 41, thirty-two-cell vertical launch system. Under each of the innocuous-looking trapdoors of the system was an assortment of deadly surface-to-surface and surface-to-air missiles, or rocket-assisted torpedoes. On the aft deck ahead of the landing pad, a sixty-four-cell vertical

launch system sat with twice as many missiles and torpedoes as the fore system contained. On either side of the
sixty-four-cell launcher were three torpedo tubes and
two Harpoon surface-to-surface missiles.

At either end of its superstructure was a Mark 15,
20mm Vulcan-Phalanx gun capable of shooting incoming missiles out of the sky, should they come danger-
ously near the destroyer. In addition to the Vulcans, the
ship had the capability of launching chaff or flares to
distract incoming missiles, and it also possessed a wide
array of electronic countermeasures. On the off-chance
that a missile should get through its defenses, steel was
used everywhere in the outer armor plate except in the
ship's aluminum funnels, and seventy tons of antiballistic Kevlar fabric had been incorporated into the vessel's
design.

Hull-mounted and towed sonar, along with
phased-array and surface-search radar, allowed the ship
to be aware of everything around, above, or below it
for some distance. In short, the small destroyer was capable of surviving a massive attack and going on the
offensive at a moment's notice.

"Are you getting used to the controls?" Death
Song asked Oz as the pilot approached the *Patrick
Henry.*

"In a word, no," Oz answered. "With the torpedoes on the wing and the new sonar dispenser, it just
doesn't feel right. I wish we had more time to work out
the kinks before we started the exercise tomorrow. But
I guess it can't be helped."

Oz circled the ship once, then matched speed with
the destroyer so the MH-60K seemed to hover over the
white circle painted on the landing pad. Still not used

to the balance of the chopper in its new configuration, he carefully lowered the collective pitch lever on the chopper, to set it on the slightly swaying ship.

O.T. and Luger squeezed around the sonobuoy dispenser that nearly filled the side doors of the MH-60K to stand by Death Song and Oz.

"I don't know about you guys," O.T. said with a grin, "but I'm already feeling sea sick."

While O.T., Death Song, and Luger were given an informal tour of the *Patrick Henry,* Oz met with the ship's captain and executive officer to go over the exercise that would be conducted the next day.

Following the meeting, Oz was taken to the mess hall and, from there, to the quarters assigned to him and his team. Though the Antarctic sun still hung high in the summer sky, the men settled down to sleep on the ship that continued to roll on the ocean swells.

Oz lay awake for some time worrying about being able to handle the helicopter with the new equipment installed on it.

The next day was full of surprises. No sooner had Oz and his crew suited up than a message came from the Joint Chiefs of Staff: the Night Stalkers and their Delta Team in Antarctica were to assist a landing party from the submarine, the USS *Oklahoma,* that had been scheduled to engage in the hide-and-seek exercise. According to the message, an emergency had arisen at a US experimental base, Anderson Station.

Oz waited nervously as the crew members of the

Patrick Henry removed the sonar equipment from his MH-60K helicopter so the chopper could be utilized to pick up the submarine's landing party and ferry them to the base.

10

Captain Frank Miller had wondered why the USS *Oklahoma* was being rerouted from its original rendezvous with the *Patrick Henry* to a new position a hundred kilometers farther south. The captain's new orders had directed him to sail south through the channel cleared by an icebreaker at the beginning of the summer to Gould Bay, Antarctica. From there, he was to receive an MH-60K helicopter so it could ferry an *armed* party to Anderson Station.

According to the brief message, Anderson Station was in trouble and had possibly been attacked. A frantic plea for help had been received and then radio contact was lost. Captain Miller's landing party was to discover what had happened and—if possible—to rectify the situation.

"What's our sounding?" Captain Miller asked.

"We have . . . fifty fathoms under our keel," his navigator answered.

"Good," Captain Miller said. No danger of running aground. He walked to the control room. "Let's look topside." The captain worried about damaging one of the fin-mounted hydroplanes by hitting the ice when they surfaced. Sonar had told him it was clear, but he preferred to see with his own eyes before giving the order to surface.

Captain Miller stepped to the periscope pedestal. "Up scope."

One of the petty officers switched the hydraulic ring control. The portside search periscope lifted smoothly from its well.

Captain Miller waited until it was well above the surface of the water. "Hold." He stepped to the conning station and placed his eyes to the scope. He blinked at the sunlit shades of blue and white where the bright sunlight was refracted through the ice and water. After his eye had adjusted to the light, he paced the scope through a full circle. As he viewed the frigid ocean, his executive officer studied the TV monitor fastened to the forward bulkhead. The monitor was coupled to the camera mounted in the periscope and showed what the captain was viewing.

"Looks clear all around," Captain Miller said.

"I concur, Skipper," Executive Officer Dodd said, nodding agreement.

"Scope down," the captain ordered. "Does sonar show any ice close to us?"

Engineering Officer Bell checked and then spoke, "Sonar still doesn't have anything around us, Skipper."

"Good. Let's surface. Mr. Dodd, delegate a couple of lookouts to accompany us. We'll guide her into the bay from the conning tower and then prepare the deck for the helicopter."

There was a flurry of activity in the control room as the sailors commenced the steps to blow the ballast tanks and surface. Air was sucked from above the water through the snorkel tube in the sail. The air was then compressed by the pumps and channeled to the main ballast where it expelled the water that served as the sub's ballast. As the water left, the submarine's deck quickly rose to the ocean's surface.

Dodd collected the two lookouts and the three stood around the skipper, waiting for his commands.

"Gentlemen," Captain Miller said to the two sailors, "I hope you remembered to put on your long underwear this morning."

Captain Frank Miller watched silently from the conning tower at the top of the "sail" as his crew finished checking the mount that would secure the cable from the MH-60K. This cable would allow the helicopter to land on the swaying submarine's deck.

The sailors labored swiftly in near silence. The antarctic sunlight bathed the Ohio-class Trident II sub that stretched 560 feet stem to stern, looking like a black mechanical whale from Captain Miller's vantage point on the conning tower.

The captain glanced at the rescue hatch on the aftdeck that would serve as the marker for the helicopter's landing platform. Like the other two hatches on the deck, it was outlined in a white circle and lines to make it easy to locate by a rescue team.

He turned and inspected the hydroplane on the side of the sail on which one of the lookouts stood studying the area with a pair of binoculars. The captain glanced at the tall periscope and antenna array to the rear of the conning tower, satisfying himself that everything was right.

"We've got the helicopter on the radar, Skipper,"

Executive Officer Dodd's voice told the captain over the intercom.

"We're ready for them up here," the captain replied after flipping the switch on the intercom. "Tell Chief Poll to talk them in—the doctor does have him patched up, doesn't he?"

"Yeah," Dodd answered. "Except for a large bandage on his hand, your radio chief is as good as new."

"We're ready to land, over," Oz radioed to the USS *Oklahoma*. The gray and black submarine sat in a wide channel broken through the ice sheet that covered most of the ocean around it.

"You're cleared to land just aft of the middle emergency hatch. Over," the sub's radio chief called.

Oz circled the submarine as he spoke, locating the white circle around the emergency hatch on the aft-deck. "We have located our landing position and are dropping our cable. Be sure to remind your crew not to handle the cable until it's grounded itself by touching the deck. With this dry Antarctic air it'll have quite a static electrical charge built up when we come in. We don't want to fry anyone."

"That's a roger," Radio Chief Poll answered with a smile. "I'm relaying your warning to the deck crew now. Over and out."

Oz watched the submarine below him through the chin window of the helicopter. The deck crew cautiously avoided the cable as it snaked down from the MH-60K. Once the cable had hit the deck, one sailor ran forward, grabbed it, and quickly secured it to a heavy lug on the USS *Oklahoma*'s skin.

"Your cable is fastened to our deck, over," the radio chief told Oz.

"All right, *Oklahoma,* we'll pull ourselves down, over and out." Oz switched to his intercom. "O.T., are you ready with the winch?"

"Roger."

"Take up the slack," Oz ordered.

Oz concentrated on slowly lowering the helicopter to the narrow, rolling deck of the submarine. The secret was to maintain just enough lift on the chopper to keep the cable taut. If Oz put too much pressure on the cable, it would break, possibly damaging the helicopter or injuring the sailors below him. Without enough pressure the helicopter could tumble as it reached the deck—with equally disastrous results.

So the pilot cautiously lowered the chopper. Little by little, the helicopter was pulled to the submarine until the MH-60K's three wheels were securely settled on the tossing submarine.

"Good job," Death Song told Oz.

"Thanks."

11

One hour and forty-five minutes later, a landing party from the USS *Oklahoma* had been ferried in the Night Stalkers' MH-60K helicopter over the icy shore to a low hill near the station. There the landing party disembarked to travel the rest of the distance to Anderson Station on foot since there was no way of knowing how hot the area around the base was. As the marines and two naval officers continued on foot, Oz and his men bird-dogged above the landing party, watching for any signs of trouble, ready to back them up with the helicopter's weapons if necessary.

Executive Officer Dodd led the party on the ground. The officer was well liked by the other crew members. Somehow he always managed to maintain a California tan, despite the months spent on submarine duty. In his thirties, Dodd had a nervous habit of jerking his head around and glancing from side to side while he talked.

The submarine's doctor, Lieutenant Brad Pageler, also accompanied the landing party. Pageler didn't have the demeanor of a doctor. His heavy parka covered his big-boned frame and balding scalp, but did nothing to hide his bulbous nose. His cheeks and neck seemed to suffer from a permanent case of razor burn and Dodd found himself wondering what the cold weather would do to the doctor's complexion.

Dodd and Pageler were surrounded by a squad of marines from the sub. The marines were taking their job seriously; they'd trudged through the snow with a no-nonsense silence and, after being dropped off by the helicopter, had rapidly spread to protective positions ringing the two naval officers. The marines held M16 rifles and FN Minimi machine guns at the ready; they wore cold-weather gear including parkas, heavy mittens, and inflated "Mickey Mouse" boots.

The party of men ascended an incline of blue-white ice as the wind carried the thumping sound of the MH-60K that circled above. Dodd was glad they didn't have to travel far in the intense cold. The wind swept a cloud of sleet across the ice and stung the executive officer's exposed skin.

The radio Dodd held crackled as Oz's voice came through. "This is NS-1 calling Oakee One."

"This is Oakee One," Dodd answered, glancing at a marine scout who had descended the hill and was softly conversing with Squad Leader Adams. A sparkling cloud of angel dust fell from the sky as Dodd listened to the radio.

"Anderson Station is just over this hill," Oz informed the ground party. "The base looks clear, but I'd suggest you let your marines go in first to be sure. We'll continue to cover your movements from the air."

"Good suggestion," Executive Officer Dodd concurred. "I'll send them in first. I'll be turning the radio over to my squad leader so you can communicate directly with him. Over."

"NS-1 over and out."

Trying to keep from shivering, Dodd turned to Squad Leader Adams and handed him the radio. "Don't stay too long or you'll have to carve us out of the ice."

"Aye, aye, sir," Adams said with a trace of a grin as he placed the radio in an oversize pocket in his parka. He turned and gave hand signals to the men around him. They quickly climbed the hill and vanished as their white uniforms blended into the snow-covered surroundings.

"Let's hike partway up the hill," Dodd suggested to the doctor beside him. "Maybe we can see what's going on."

"Anything's better than standing still," Lieutenant Pageler replied. "I only wish I'd drunk a little more antifreeze before we started."

The two Navy officers climbed the hill and crouched alongside a high drift to protect themselves from the wind and to keep out of sight of the base. From their vantage point, the officers were able to spy on the station that lay nearly a kilometer ahead of them.

From the air Oz could see that something had gone very wrong at the base. The central dome had a gaping hole in it.

"Anyone see anything moving down there?" he asked over the intercom.

All the crew answered in the negative. Oz switched to the radio and triggered it on. "NS-1 to Oakee One."

"This is Oakee One," the voice of Squad Leader Adams answered.

"There's no activity at the station, over."

"Thanks, NS-1. We're getting ready to head in now."

"That's a roger. Over and out."

"Arm the guns and rocket pods," Oz ordered Death Song. "Luger, O.T., heads up, the marines are going in now."

Oz circled the base, watching the soldiers as they neared one of the outlying domes.

Squad Leader Adams gave the signal for his men to stop as they neared the Anderson Station complex. He pulled his radio from his pocket and thumbed it on. Suddenly he realized how exposed their position was: a brunette brandishing a pistol in her hand wandered outside from the central dome and pointed the gun directly at Adams.

"We're Americans," Adams yelled. "Here to help. Please drop the gun."

For a moment the marine thought his voice had been lost in the wind since the woman didn't seem to have heard. But then she screamed an answer, "No way, you filthy bastards. You killed my little sister, but you'll never capture me." Her bare hands shook as she fired blindly, almost as if she were unable to determine where the American marines were, although they were right in front of her.

"Hold your fire," Adams hollered to his men. The marine squad leader didn't want to shoot the American woman if he could avoid it. "Stay behind the drift," he ordered his men.

The woman fired three more shots without aiming into the snow-covered expanse encircling her. With her last shot the slide locked back on her automatic pistol. The woman swore, throwing the empty pistol away as she scampered to a nearby snow tractor.

"Shall we fire or let her escape?" one of the marines asked Adams.

Adams tried to decide what to do as the tractor's engine coughed, then cranked up with a loud thumping roar. Adams didn't want to injure the unarmed woman—after all, they had been sent to protect any survivors on the base. Yet letting the woman escape after she had fired on the troops hardly seemed right. And it was even possible that she might be a trespasser rather than a member of the station.

Adams came to a quick decision. "Let her leave. We'll let the helicopter head her off and pick her up if she gets too far." He was abruptly aware of the radio in his hand and glanced at the MH-60K that continued to circle above them.

Adams prepared to call the helicopter as the tractor started moving. But the vehicle didn't turn to leave the base. Instead, it veered in a quarter circle, plowing through a drift of snow, and headed toward the American marines.

Adams turned to his machine gunner. "Fire a warning shot in front of her on my command. The rest of you hold your fire." He turned to the Minimi gunner. "Fire," he ordered.

The machine gunner discharged a short burst. Adams was surprised to see how little snow was kicked into the air by the bullets thumping into the snow in front of the tractor.

The woman should have the sense to turn away from the armed men standing in front of her, Adams told himself. But instead, she continued at a breakneck pace toward the marines.

"All fire!" Adams ordered as the vehicle continued its charge toward them.

The squad's M16 rifles, along with the Minimi, chewed into the tractor, spalding large holes in the windshield and pocking its metal skin with .22-caliber holes. The vehicle came to a grinding halt as the woman slumped behind the controls.

A single soldier continued his salvo.

"Cease fire!" Adams ordered. Then, by hand signals, he designated two of his men to follow him.

The three marines charged toward the tractor with rifles held in the assault position, stocks tucked under their arms. As Adams neared the door, he motioned the soldiers to either side of him. "Cover the door."

The marines shouldered their rifles, pointing the weapons toward the tractor. Adams intently watched the motionless silhouette of the woman, barely visible through the frost-covered side window. He grasped the door handle, turned it, and jerked it open. He didn't need to check to see if the woman inside was dead. One glimpse of her broken temple told him she was.

Adams slammed the door in anger. "Why the hell did she try to ram us?" he demanded. It irked him that they had been forced to kill the woman. The marines milling around the squad leader remained silent.

A moment later Adams had bridled his emotions and regrouped his men. "All right, let's proceed toward the center dome. Keep your eyes open. There may be more crazies, and with all our shooting, they'll damned well know we're here.

"We're proceeding to the dome," Adams said into his radio.

"Roger, we'll continue circling the base. Everything looks clear from up here."

After what seemed hours, the MH-60K thundered down from nowhere to land in front of Dodd on the ridge above Anderson Station. The chopper's blades whipped up a storm of loose ice and snow.

"Sir," O.T. said as he jogged up to Dodd and Pageler, "the station's clear."

Executive Officer Dodd walked alongside O.T. as he returned to the chopper. "What was the shooting about?" Dodd asked. "Did you run into trouble?"

"They had a little trouble on the ground," O.T. answered. "Some lady attacked them with a pistol. When she ran out of shells, she tried to run them down with one of those tracked vehicles."

"Didn't they alert her that they were there to help?" Pageler asked.

"We could hear the commotion over the radio. Your squad leader told her they were there to help. And they held their fire until the last minute. But the lady didn't seem to understand. There don't appear to be any other survivors."

Dodd, Pageler, and O.T. climbed into the MH-60K. Oz lifted the chopper into the air and they headed to the base.

After contacting Adams to determine that there was still no problem on the ground, Oz delivered Executive Officer Dodd and the submarine's doctor to the cleared area north of the central dome. The chopper then lifted back into the air to circle the base and act as a lookout until the marines determined what had caused the deaths in the station.

Dodd entered the large central dome. The huge chamber was unheated—a large drift of snow had formed under the hole blown in its surface—but it was considerably warmer than outside, thanks to its shelter from the wind.

"We just found a survivor," Squad Leader Adams told Dodd as he entered the dome. "We haven't moved her. She's unconscious."

Dodd turned to the doctor.

"I'll see what I can do." Pageler unbuckled the strap that held the medical kit on his back.

Executive Officer Dodd followed the doctor and Adams. He was horrified by what he saw inside the dome. Station personnel were sprawled about the floor of the large dome. Most had massive wounds, their blood frozen in black pools around their bodies. One appeared to have been beaten to a pulp.

Dodd glanced away, trying not to look too closely at the bodies.

They entered a long cave of crystalline snow lit by a blue glow from the sunlight filtering through the thick ice. Dodd's feet kicked empty brass casings as he walked; ahead of him was another cluster of bodies, lying frozen on the floor.

As he passed, Dodd noted that each man had a head wound, several with portions of their faces or scalps blown open. "What the hell happened here?" he asked, stepping through the door frame at the end of the tunnel.

"Near as we can tell," Adams answered, his voice echoing in the large chamber, "there was a battle down here. But the weird thing of it is, they're all members of the station. We haven't a clue where the attackers came from. The shell casings seem to have come from American weapons, too."

Pageler knelt on the tiled floor and leaned over the woman stretched out on it. She had a large gash on her forehead. Blood caked her hair and a dried pool on the floor looked like a black halo.

"Why aren't the bodies in here frozen like those outside?" Dodd asked. Then he glanced at the dials and instruments on the walls of the chamber. "This their reactor?"

"Yes, sir," Adams answered. "That's why she didn't freeze. The nuclear pile kept this area warm. It looks like it's shut down, but the fuel still generates heat."

Dodd turned toward the doctor. He was holding smelling salts under the woman's nose. She groaned and her eyes fluttered open.

"It's okay," Dr. Pageler told her as she struggled weakly to free herself from his grasp. "I'm a doctor and we're here to help you." Garrett quit struggling.

The doctor removed a penlight from his bag and switched it on. He studied her eyes; both pupils constricted in the sudden light.

"You don't have a concussion, anyway," he told her. "You are running a temperature, according to this hi-tech electric thermometer. You may be suffering from an infection from your wound."

The doctor glanced at Dodd as he spoke. "I'd prefer to transport her back to the boat at once. I need to run some tests. Hell, our men are going to be suffering from exposure if we stay out much longer. This is the only halfway warm place we've been in for an hour—and it's nearly freezing in here."

"Miss, uh," Dodd read the name tag on the woman's snowsuit. "Garrett. Can you tell us what happened here?"

The woman shook her head, then spoke in a croaking voice. "Everyone. Everyone went crazy."

"But who attacked the base?"

She shook her head. "No one."

"But how—"

"They just went crazy," Garrett insisted. She closed her eyes.

Dodd raised an eyebrow and studied Dr. Pageler.

The doctor shrugged as if to say that he couldn't tell whether she was hallucinating or telling the truth.

"Let's radio the chopper and have them return you two to the *Oklahoma*," Dodd said to the doctor. "The rest of us will check to be sure everyone's accounted for and then return after the helicopter comes back for us. In the meantime maybe we can find out what happened around here."

12

Dodd and the marines unearthed nothing to explain how or why the massacre had occurred. A log discovered in the commander's quarters enabled them to account for the members of the station—all but one: Dr. Peter Mikhalsky. The soldiers found no sign of the Russian scientist. The Antarctic storm was breaking over the area when Dodd and the marines returned to the safety of the USS *Oklahoma*.

"Can you make it back to the *Patrick Henry?*" Radio Chief Poll called to Oz after the last of the marines had climbed from the helicopter sitting on the swaying deck of the submarine.

Oz couldn't see that they had much choice but to try to make it back. He decided not to burden the submarine officer with his troubles, however. "We should make it without any problem," he answered instead. "I suspect we can climb above the storm and then outrun it before it reaches the ship."

"All right then, we won't keep you. Good luck. Over."

"Thanks, *Oklahoma*. Be seeing you in the exercise tomorrow."

"Not if we can help it! We aim to stay hidden from your sonar. Over and out."

Oz fought his chopper into the air and then struggled to get them above the wind that buffeted the MH-60K.

Captain Frank Miller watched from the conning tower as the MH-60K was lost in the howling winds. He regretted having to force the chopper crew to leave in such weather, but saw no way to avoid it. He pushed the thought from his mind as Dodd climbed up to stand beside him.

"All hatches are secure on deck, Captain Miller."

"Let's be on our way then," Miller said evenly as he studied the sky. "The sooner we get under, the better."

"Deck crew below," Dodd hollered to the four men still on the swaying surface of the submarine.

The sailors were bent over in the wind. They carefully made their way across the slick deck toward the doors at either side of the sail's base.

"Go down and take the control room, Mr. Dodd. Prepare to dive."

"Aye, aye, Captain."

Dodd left the conning tower, slowly descending the ladder inside the sail, and then slipped through the hatch of the pressure hull. The control room was lit with its red surface lights, giving the crew members in the room a surreal cast.

The gray-green equipment consoles lining the control room were in stark contrast to submarines of just a few decades before. This boat was automated and computerized; a flow-chart style made many of the instruments simple to control from the console.

Engineering Officer Bell glanced at Dodd as he entered the control room. Standing next to the helmsman, Bell was quiet, as usual. He had one green and one blue eye and light blond hair that gave him a ghostly albino appearance. Bell was very competent at his job and well respected by the other crewmen.

"How is she, Mr. Bell?" Dodd asked.

"She's running great, Mr. Dodd," the engineering officer replied.

"I'll take her now," Dodd instructed.

"Very good, sir."

Dodd positioned himself at the console, carefully studying the readings of the equipment around him. "Let's prepare to dive."

There was a flurry of activity initiated by Dodd's order. Instruments were checked and double-checked and gear stowed.

In three minutes the submarine was prepared to dive. Dodd relayed his message from the control room through the sail's speaker in the conning tower next to Miller. "We're prepared to dive and awaiting your order, Captain."

"Very good, Mr. Dodd." The captain turned from the intercom. "Lookouts below," he ordered the cold sailors standing on the hydroplanes on the port and starboard. The men crept off the winglike appendages and climbed the hand rungs on the side of the sail. Once in the conning tower, they carefully removed their icy safety lines and scrambled down the ladder inside the sail. The captain visually inspected the submarine and then gave his order, "Ahead one-third."

"Ahead one-third," Dodd's voice echoed on the intercom.

The USS *Oklahoma* shuddered slightly as it slid silently along the channel, its huge, seven-bladed propeller noiselessly shoving the boat through the murky water. The boat began to accelerate, making its own wave of water that washed over the bow, across the deck, and splashed against the base of the sail. The wave streamed along the deck and back over the barely discernible ports aft of the conning tower where the twenty-four Trident II D-5 missiles were hidden in their launch tubes. The wave then continued, etching a V in the water that lapped up on the ice surrounding the channel.

Miller eyed the hatches on the launch tubes. Each of the submarine-launched ballistic missiles in the tubes carried a multiple warhead capable of being targeted to eight different locations. Every one of the warheads packed a one-hundred-kiloton punch—equal to one hundred thousand pounds of TNT. For a moment the captain was nearly overwhelmed by the power he controlled in the submarine that had cost the American taxpayers nearly two billion dollars.

The USS *Oklahoma* continued to accelerate. As Captain Miller watched, the deck dropped beneath the ocean's surface so only the sail remained free of the water. The captain called down through the intercom, "Take her on down, Mr. Dodd."

The captain climbed down the conning tower's inner ladder, carefully dogging the pressure hatch shut before descending into the control room. "Sail and pressure hull hatches are secured, Mr. Dodd."

"Very well, Captain."

"How's it look, Mr. Hudson?" the captain asked the diving officer.

"Straight board, Captain Miller."

"Let's take her to one hundred meters, Mr. Dodd."

Dodd relayed the order.

Crewmen set the fin and aft hydroplanes to their dive positions and opened the vents, letting water flood into the boat's main ballast tank. The swaying and rocking of the USS *Oklahoma* decreased as it sank into the water where the waves no longer influenced it. The control room was silent except for the rumblings of the huge machine in which the men were encased.

Since descending at too steep an angle could be dangerous, the speed of descent was soon checked by adjusting the hydroplanes back to their raised position. Finally, the announcement was made: "One hundred meters, sir."

The captain turned to the engineering officer. "Mr. Bell, how do you read her?"

Bell quickly glanced at his instrumental display. "Nominal, Captain."

"Good. Mr. Dodd, let's turn her around and take her back to sea. When you leave the bay, let's take her on down to five hundred meters proximate, standard speed."

"Aye, Aye, Captain."

The captain surveyed the control room.

"Take the conn, Mr. Dodd."

"Aye, aye, sir."

"I'm going to see how our patient is doing and see if Doc has gotten any information from her," the captain told Dodd. "I'll relieve you when I return. Then

I want you to make a full report of your trip so I can send it stateside when we resurface."

"Aye, aye, Skipper," Dodd said. As the captain left Dodd wondered if any of them would ever know exactly what had happened at Anderson Station.

13

When the USS *Oklahoma* reached the open sea, it again resurfaced and, via satellite, radioed its bizarre findings at Anderson Station to the US Naval Command. An hour and fifteen minutes later, after the message had passed through the chain of command, the submarine was ordered to resume its scheduled exercises in the Weddell Sea and then transfer Dr. Grace Garrett ashore during the next scheduled stop, since she did not seem to be seriously injured.

"So what do you think happened there?" Captain Miller asked the submarine's chief medical officer as he and Executive Officer Dodd sat at the compact table in the officers' wardroom.

Dr. Pageler set a Styrofoam cup full of steaming coffee down on the table. "Garrett—the lady we brought aboard—doesn't seem to know anything. She's still claiming that everyone acted like they were in the nuthouse. She also claims they'd had the flu or bad colds—she's still running a fever and I'm keeping her in the sick bay and completing a battery of lab tests just in case. But no flu causes its victims to go insane."

"Then what happened?" the captain asked. "Any theories?"

"Well, if just one or two of them had gone bonkers," the doctor replied, nursing the coffee cup in his hands, "I'd chalk it up to cabin fever."

"It had to be an attack on the base," Dodd said.

"But then why weren't there any signs of an outside force?" the captain asked. "No enemy bodies—"

"Or even blood, as far as we could tell," Dodd interrupted. "I'll admit it was damned peculiar. But what else explains it?"

"Is there any way Garrett could be telling the truth?" the captain asked the doctor.

The doctor deliberated for a moment. "Well, this situation has all the elements of classic paranoia, taken to its most extreme."

"But doesn't paranoia usually affect only one person at a time?" the captain asked.

"Not always." The doctor paused and took another sip from his cup. "Paranoia is a curious mental state. It can infect entire communities or even countries—Nazi Germany being a prime example. Or the Americans and Soviets during the height of the Cold War. There are conditions when paranoia can spread quickly and encompass entire communities."

"But wouldn't they be aware of what was happening?" Executive Office Dodd asked.

"Not necessarily," the doctor answered. "I'm no psychiatrist, but they do teach us a little about such things before sealing us up at sea for seventy days tending one hundred forty-seven sex-starved men in a—"

"We get the point," the captain said dryly.

"Yeah. So anyway," the doctor continued, "unlike

many other mental and physical diseases, paranoia has the uncommon quality of rarely being recognized by those suffering from it."

"I'm normal; it's everyone else who's crazy," the captain suggested.

"Exactly."

"But how could the whole station go crazy at the same time?" Dodd asked with disbelief.

"Maybe not all of them," Pageler suggested. "Just key personnel. All you'd need are a few people displaying such tendencies to make everything come apart at the seams."

"What triggers such behavior?" the captain asked.

"That'd be one for the full-time shrinks," Pageler said. "But it could be triggered by just a minor disagreement. When you're cooped up as they were at the station and the length of the day/night periods screws up your circadian cycles . . . Some bad food, the world news—some little thing—might trigger it. Of course—"

"Lieutenant Pageler," the intercom in the room interrupted.

The doctor stood and pressed the talk button. "Pageler here."

"Doc, we've got problems in sick bay. That broad we took aboard tried to beat the medic to death with a food tray. He'll be needing some stitches. And four marines are on sick call with fevers."

"I'll be there in a moment." The doctor turned toward the captain. "Captain, I suggest you contact Naval Command at once. I'm betting we've contracted Anderson Station's flu or whatever the bug is. It may be nothing, but given the conditions at the station and Garrett's behavior now . . ."

"I'll do so at once. Now get to sick bay," Captain Miller urged.

"Aye, aye, Captain."

14

The source of Major Churkin Novikov's troubles had been conceived a few years after he'd been born. The problems had then taken three decades to catch up with him. Now that they'd caught him, they had rolled over him like cold ocean waves trying to drown him.

He slouched in his white, snow-camouflage uniform that was emblazoned with a starred brass belt buckle and medals from his campaign in Afghanistan. He pushed himself out from behind his scuffed metal desk, rolling backward on the old East German office chair as he blew a cloud of foul-smelling pipe smoke into the air.

Novikov watched the smoke stratify in the air as he listened to the Antarctic wind that howled mournfully outside the metal building. The sound set his teeth on edge.

And this miserable head cold, he thought, blowing his noise on a stained handkerchief. The whole base was sick with the cold.

Except for the illness, Novikov's problems stemmed from a treaty his country had signed with the United States and ten other nations in 1959; the document had delayed the settlement of Antarctica for thirty years. The treaty lapsed in 1989, coinciding with Premier Gorbachev's reforms—one of which was to reduce the activities of the Spetsnaz. The expiration of the treaty made it convenient for the Supreme Soviet to start a new wave of Antarctic explorations and colonizations—manned by troops that had become an embarrassment to the media-conscious leader.

So just as Novikov's military career had begun to look promising, the Brigada Osobovo Naznacheniya units of the Spetsnaz had been broken up, and his remnant of men had suffered the fate of being sent to the frigid wasteland at the bottom of the world. Here he sat in the Soyez III station west of the Korff Ice Rise on the Ronne Ice Shelf with nothing to do, nowhere to go.

No wonder my troops refer to Antarctica as the "New Siberia," he thought as he tapped the pipe on the old sardine can that was his ashtray. He wiped his nose again, wondering why everyone at the base seemed to have caught the same cold.

Major Novikov's thoughts returned to the task at hand. He felt he finally had a chance to derail the downward path of his career. Maybe even succeed in getting his country back on the road to strength and power, so it wouldn't have to continue to grovel for handouts from the West. He refilled his pipe, lit it, and puffed it to life. He exhaled another cloud of smoke, pondering his options.

The opportunity for changing things had come in the form of another Russian. The major decided the man's nationality was a good omen, even if the man himself was a soft intellectual who had been working with the Americans. Novikov's soldiers had found the scientist during a routine patrol. He had been lying in an American snow vehicle, nearly dead from exposure. The patrol had brought the man to the Soyez III where the base's medic had revived him.

Even though the Russian scientist had been rescued from death, he had still seemed disoriented. "All this babbling about a whole American station going crazy." Novikov laughed to himself, shaking his head. And yet there somehow seemed to be a grain of truth in Mikhalsky's story—and that was what Novikov had to puzzle out.

There was no doubt that Mikhalsky had left the base with an American vehicle. And no effort had been made by the US to find him, as far as Novikov could tell. That was puzzling in itself; the Americans prided themselves on their abilities to rescue stranded whales and lost fools. Furthermore, monitoring of the American station had revealed that all radio traffic had ceased.

Novikov had contacted his command at the Second Military Directorate of Soviet Military Intelligence to alert them that something strange was going on. But their disappointing response was for him to sit tight and do nothing.

Novikov swore a long string of curses that encompassed *glasnost* and Soviet bureaucrats. Finally he'd exhausted his anger. He set his pipe aside and poured more vodka into the dirty glass in front of him.

If my teachers could see me now, he thought. Nearly an alcoholic, his hands tied, unable to help his motherland. And his Spetsnaz troops, once the pride of the USSR, trained to bring down the corrupt armies of the capitalists . . . they'd been reduced to baby-sitting a pack of scientists and castoffs in the cold wasteland of Antarctica.

And all the while, an American base seemed to sit ripe for the picking, a few kilometers away.

Novikov was sure there was something strange going on at the American base. Orders or not, the major decided he was going to discover what it was.

15

The flulike disease brought from Anderson Station had quickly spread through the USS *Oklahoma*. Only after every third man was ill did the boat's maintenance personnel discover that the air filter to the ventilation system had been left out.

Had the filter been in place, Dr. Pageler mused, the disease might have been checked. Instead, chances were good that everyone was going to come down with symptoms, varying from sniffles to a high fever and chills. Currently, most of the crew members were able to continue their duties; only a few required bed rest.

But Pageler didn't think that was going to continue. Not if his tests of Dr. Garrett proved to be correct.

Pageler glanced at his patient. She glared back at Pageler.

Garrett had attacked Pageler's orderly and more recently had refused to speak or eat. Pageler had been forced not only to strap her into a medical bed but to put her through the indignities of a catheter as well. Since she refused to eat, he'd been compelled to order a tube of glucose to be fed into a vein in her arm. Now her glaring eyes did little to soothe his conscience.

At least she's stopped her screaming, Pageler thought. If she'd known how that was getting to everyone, she'd have kept it up. Instead, she'd settled for trying to kill them with her eyes.

"Well, Dr. Garrett," Pageler said, replacing her chart at the base of the bed. "I can appreciate the fact that you don't think I'm trying to help you get better. But I am. And I believe I've turned up something with my latest battery of tests. In fact, I'm surprised that I didn't discover it earlier. You, and the rest of the *Oklahoma*'s crew, I suspect, are suffering from a bacterial infection—not a viral disease. And *that* we can cure with an antibiotic. So I have one more indignity to heap upon you. Then—I hope—your condition will improve and you'll come to your senses."

She launched into one of her tirades, "Fat chance, you stupid, retarded donkey's—"

"You don't happen to know if you're allergic to penicillin G, do you?" Pageler interrupted.

She struggled against her bonds, then gave up and renewed her efforts to bore holes into him with her eyes.

The doctor filled a hypodermic syringe from a vial he'd taken from the medical cabinet. He tapped the bubbles to the base of the hollow needle, then expelled them with a gentle push of the plunger.

The doctor drew down the thin sheet that covered Garrett and rubbed an area on her upper thigh with a cleansing pad. He tried to ignore the beautiful curves in her thigh as he expertly jabbed the needle into the rectus femoris muscle of the front of her leg and pumped the contents of the syringe into it.

He slid the cleansing pad over the needle hole after extracting the syringe, staving the tiny dot of blood that appeared. He carefully rubbed her taut muscle, massaging the antibiotic into it, again aware of how beautiful her legs were.

"I'll check on you in a couple of hours. I suspect we may already notice a change by then." He covered her with the sheet and then tucked it in around her shoulders. "In the meantime I'll have an orderly observe you to be sure you don't have an allergic reaction to the antibiotic."

Her eyes continued to blaze as he left the sick bay.

Pageler stepped into the narrow metal corridor of the submarine and spied Captain Miller. "Skipper."

"Lieutenant Pageler," the captain said, pausing for the doctor to catch up with him.

"Skipper, I think I've discovered what's wrong with Garrett."

"I thought we already knew. She's crazy, isn't she?"

"Well, yes and no. I think her insane behavior is precipitated by a bacterial infection that's causing some damage to her nervous system. Similar to the type that causes acute bacterial meningitis. The symptoms are a little different; instead of nausea and merely being irritable, victims seem to exhibit flulike symptoms and manic or paranoid behavior—the same extreme behavior that apparently took place at Anderson Station."

"Contagious?" the captain asked.

The doctor nodded. "Very. And it seems to have

an extremely short incubation time—a matter of hours."

"Then you're suggesting that the cold most of the crew has is actually . . ."

"Right. But the good news is that my tests show a readily available antibiotic should knock it out. I'm trying penicillin on Garrett now. In the meantime I think we should proceed to the nearest port since we don't have enough of this type of antibiotic to treat more than twenty or thirty crew members. I'd also suggest that we inoculate you and some of our key personnel as soon as we see if Garrett improves."

"I don't know about inoculating anybody right now."

"If we try to keep our rendezvous with the *Patrick Henry* and *Thomas Jefferson* tomorrow," the doctor insisted, "I'm convinced the same thing will happen on the *Oklahoma* that Dodd and I saw at Anderson Station."

"Are you sure the disease really causes madness?"

"Well, not totally. Not until I see the effect the antibiotic has on Garrett. But—"

"Then we should at least wait until you know something for sure. And we can't take the *Oklahoma* into port yet for sure. How would I look if I jumped out of the exercise without any real reason?"

"Yeah, I suppose we can't head for port just because there *might* be a problem. But I think this could get serious real fast. The exercise isn't all that important. We don't want to—"

"Keep me advised," Captain Miller said, checking his watch. "But until you've got firm evidence, I've got to keep us on patrol. I'll see you later."

The captain strode down the corridor, leaving Pageler behind wondering why the threat to the sub wasn't being taken more seriously. Better get back to work, Pageler finally decided. Leave the decisions to the captain.

A half hour later Captain Miller called Dodd to the skipper's stateroom, just forward of the control room. The small room contained the captain's bed, a sink, and a private head.

Dodd paused in front of the open door.

"Come on in, Dodd," Captain Miller said. "And close the door behind you. Sit down."

Dodd sat uncomfortably in the chair offered him, wondering why the captain looked so serious.

Captain Miller locked unblinking eyes on the executive officer. "Dodd, I've always felt I could trust you."

"Yes, sir. And I've always trusted you, too, sir," Dodd said, hoping his voice sounded more sincere to the captain than it did to him.

The captain stared at Dodd for what seemed to the executive officer like several minutes before speaking. "In the past I've joked with you about fighting the Soviets. But there's always an element of truth in such jokes. For years we were a hair trigger away from an all-out nuclear war.

"Despite the apparent warming of relations between the East and West, the Soviets still pose a definite threat to the US. Perhaps more so than ever before, since our country has been diverting money away from the military. And the Russians haven't dismantled all that many tanks or missiles."

"Yes, sir. It's not like the USSR has completely disarmed or anything. I've always supposed our being on patrol is quite important to the safety of the United States."

"Damned right, Dodd. And you're familiar with how our government has been giving free handouts to the Soviets as well as the other communists—most of whom now call themselves social democrats—in Eastern Europe."

"Yes, sir, sometimes it seems like we help them stay on their feet so they can keep posing a threat and competing with us."

"Exactly. Sometimes I feel like Joe McCarthy was right. It seems like Washington goes out of its way to help communist governments." The captain stood and paced the room for a moment, his hands locked behind his back. Suddenly he stopped and rubbed his aching head, sat down abruptly, and nervously tugged at his earlobe. "Well, you know what I think?"

"Uh, no, sir."

"And this is between you and me."

"Of course, sir."

"I think the US Government is actually under the control of the Soviets."

Dodd didn't move, unsure how to react to what Miller had suggested to him. Again, the executive officer had the uneasy feeling that the captain expected something of him, but he had no idea what it was. Dodd pulled a tissue from his pocket and wiped his nose, hoping he wouldn't have to blow it in the captain's presence.

Captain Miller didn't seem to notice Dodd's discomfort. He rose and paced the tiny room again, speaking as he walked.

"This may seem farfetched to you," the captain continued. "But that's the cunningness of the whole thing. Just imagine that even though the Soviets seem to have lost the Cold War, it was really us Americans who lost instead. Imagine that those subs they had off our coast during the eighties were the basis of secret blackmail: surrender or we'll wipe New York and Washington off the map. Do you understand what I'm saying?"

"Our leaders decide it's better to surrender rather than have so many Americans slaughtered by an attack we aren't prepared to defend ourselves against . . ."

"Right. We didn't have any antiballistic missiles or viable civil defense for our people."

"And our surrender would explain the aid that we now give to the Soviets and Chinese."

"But it wouldn't be aid . . ." the captain let his voice trail off.

"Rather, it would be the spoils of war."

"Exactly, Dodd. It's the only thing that can really explain the recent economic aid and military concessions the president and Congress have made to the Russians. It explains why we're helping the USSR's crumbling empire and their sad economy. The public is fooled and the real patriots—like you and me—continue our duties, unaware of what's really going on."

Dodd deliberated, wishing his head didn't hurt so much. "It does make sense . . . But how—what—can we do?"

"I have an idea. We can start operating on our own—just for a few days," Miller suggested. "See what happens. If the Soviets are in control, they'll panic at the thought of twenty-four Trident missiles out of their influence and under the control of men willing to fight for their country's freedom."

Dodd was confused. What the captain was suggesting would have been unthinkable to him a few days before. Yet now it seemed to make perfect sense.

"That would turn up the heat on those sneaky bastards," Dodd finally said. The captain's idea was sounding better and better to him.

"But we'll have to be careful," Miller continued. "I think we have Soviet spies on board."

Dodd nodded. "That's probable. Spies would be a good way to keep control of any American sub. Put a spy or two on board to keep us from acting on our own if we ever catch on to what's happened."

"Exactly." The captain smiled and looked into space for a moment. Then he turned back to Dodd and whispered, "And I think I know who the spy is on the *Oklahoma.*" He paused and leaned to within inches of Dodd's face. "Lieutenant Pageler."

"The doc?" Dodd asked.

Captain Miller straightened up.

"That would make sense, I guess," Dodd agreed. "Who'd ever suspect the chief medic?"

Dodd nodded.

"And a few minutes ago he tried to get us to go to the nearest port with some cockamamie story that this cold we're all suffering from is a disease that's going to make us all crazy. Hell, I've never felt more sane in my entire life."

"And," Dodd added, "it was Doc who wanted us to believe that Anderson Station had suffered from some type of paranoia rather than an actual attack."

The captain nodded. "You thought it was an attack

on the station, didn't you? I'll bet that bastard was trying to cover it up by saying it was a disease rather than an attack. Now he's trying to twist things further to get us to port. And I'd be willing to bet I'll be relieved of my command if he succeeds in getting us to dock and then makes his secret little report to his superiors."

"Do you think he suspects that you know the truth?"

"It's possible. Of course this is all between you and me. I don't know who else we can trust on the *Oklahoma*."

"Yes, Skipper. Just between you and me."

"I think they're trying to keep us out here spinning our wheels with exercises with that antiterrorist team. Submarine-chasing Army helicopters! It's ridiculous."

"Yes, sir, it is."

"I think we should put them to the test. Leave our assigned path. What do you think about that?"

Dodd thought for a moment. "I think we should do it."

"Then you'll help me discover if our country has come under communist control?"

Dodd stood, his muscles taut as if he were at attention. "Captain, you can count on me."

Miller paced the room again, then stopped. "Okay, then. We'll depart from our assigned course in thirty minutes."

"Aye, aye, Captain."

CHAPTER

16

Oz had managed to lift the MH-60K above the oncoming storm. He'd fought the high winds all the way back to the *Patrick Henry* and succeded in landing just before the storm of blowing sleet arrived.

The pilot climbed from the helicopter with a splitting headache and a runny nose. He felt himself growing more and more angry as he crossed the destroyer's swaying deck and entered the warm corridor leading toward the cabin assigned to the four helicopter crewmen.

"That damned captain tried to kill us," Oz muttered as the ship rocked under his feet. "He waited until the last minute to let us leave the submarine."

O.T. glanced at Oz, startled by this unexpected outburst. "I don't know, sir. It seemed like he was only—"

"He tried to kill us!" Oz closed his eyes. "I've got a whale of a headache. I don't know what's wrong . . ."

"Let's head for sick bay," O.T. said. "Luger's looking bad and Death Song was a little green around the gills before we left the sub."

"I'm not green around the gills, you fat tub of lard," Death Song sneered at the warrant officer.

O.T. stopped and stared at Death Song and then Oz. "Look, you two. I want you to think a minute. Remember how that lady we found at the base said everyone was sick with a cold? And then they started attacking each other . . . Remember that?"

"She was just babbling. She was completely mad," Oz said evenly. "I don't see what that has to do with the captain of the *Oklahoma* trying to kill us."

"It has everything to do with it!" O.T. said, holding Oz by the arm. "It's happening to you. Stop and consider it. You've never acted like this in all the years I've known you. Think about it."

Oz was silent.

"Now come on," O.T. said. "Let's get to the sick bay."

"I don't know what it is," the medic said after looking at Oz's throat. "Looks like a bacterial infection, though. Stuff spreads like wildfire on a ship in a cold climate like we're in now. Just to be on the safe side, I'm giving all four of you a shot of ampicillin. Roll up your sleeves, I'll be back in a moment."

"No way I'm going to get a shot," Oz whispered to O.T. "This is stupid. Let's get out of here."

17

"We've lost a nuclear submarine!" President Robert Crane bellowed to the admiral standing in front of him in the Oval Office.

"We've only lost contact with the submarine," Admiral White said meekly, visibly paling at the president's reaction to the news that a submarine had failed to report and might even be lost at sea.

"Chances are good it's a glitch in the system," Bill Yaeger, the secretary of defense, suggested.

The president pulled his robe around himself and then hit the button on his intercom. "Get Taylor in here at once." President Crane then did his best to ignore the naval officer and the defense secretary. He turned and stared out the window into the darkness that was mitigated by the hint of dawn.

The president had aged little since his second term had begun. There was only a little more gray in his hairline, a few more lines around his eyes, and an ulcer that occasionally acted up. This was the first real crisis he'd faced during his second term.

And it might be nothing, he tried to reassure himself. He turned away from the window as he heard the door click open and then latch shut.

"Yes, Mr. President," Taylor said as he entered the room. The weasel-faced man was dressed in jeans and a windbreaker rather than his usual gray pin-striped suit. Now the president's secretary of state, Taylor was a former academic who had fallen in love with the political infighting at the State Department.

"We've lost a nuclear submarine," the president told Taylor. "Ohio class. I'm assuming it has the usual complement of SLBMs, Admiral?"

"Yes, sir. Twenty-four missiles with the usual MIRVed warheads installed on each—"

The president swore. "In short, enough armament to completely destroy for all practical purposes any nation on earth. And we don't even know where the damn thing is."

"I really don't think we have any cause to worry yet," Defense Secretary Yaeger interposed.

"You must be a little worried to get me out of bed at five in the morning."

"Yes, sir. But we've only lost track of the submarine. It isn't like terrorists have it or anything."

"If *anything* has happened it will be real bad," Taylor said. "Where was it last heard from?"

"It made a call outside Gould Bay, in Antarctica," the admiral quickly replied. "Some trouble it had been sent to investigate. Then it was supposed to move out into the Weddell Sea for some training exercises with some Army choppers later this morning."

"Taylor, that's not where that base had all that trouble, is it?" the president asked.

The secretary of state rubbed his unshaven face as

he spoke. "Yes, sir, if memory serves me correctly, Gould Bay is near Anderson Station. We sent a sub in to check on what had happened. But—"

"My God," the admiral said. "Then this is the same submarine that was rerouted to check on the station. We don't have any others traveling that far south—"

"Didn't you know about the station?" the president asked the admiral in disbelief.

"I came here as soon as I heard the sub was overdue for contact," the admiral said, fighting to keep from wiping the sweat off his upper lip. "I didn't wait for a complete briefing. Most of my personnel aren't in yet this early."

"Damn," the president said. "We need to keep our information better coordinated. So what are we doing to ascertain what went wrong at the station, Yaeger?"

"We don't have much in the area now," Secretary Yaeger said. "We do have a Delta Team training near there now. We could round up a group of doctors from the Centers for Disease Control and have them down there in a hurry to try to determine what happened."

"Why the doctors?" the president asked.

"Well, the submarine's report mentioned some type of disease that had swept the station in addition to apparent fighting. The submarine's doctor thought the two might be connected. A later transmission said that several of the party that visited the station had fallen ill as well. Now we've lost them."

"So they might have contracted the same disease at the station?" the president asked. "Is that what we're talking about?"

"Yes, sir."

"How soon can you get them to the station?" the president asked.

"Within forty-eight hours. The CDC has a special troubleshooting team."

"Two days?" the president asked. The room was silent. "I want them there quicker."

"Yes, sir."

"And you keep me informed on what they find when they finally get there," the president ordered. "In the meantime I want that submarine found. I'm always hearing about how good your guys are at finding enemy submarines," the president said, turning to the admiral. "Let's see how quickly you can locate one of our own."

"It may not be easy," the admiral said uncomfortably.

"What do you mean?" the president asked.

"We only have one other sub in the area. Our fleets are too far away . . . It'd take almost half a month to get a real sub-chasing unit into position. About all we have are the two destroyers that were supposed to go through the exercise with the *Oklahoma* and an attack submarine."

"So we'll have the other submarine and the destroyers find it," the president said.

"Sir, Soviet submarines are noisy," the admiral explained. "They're easy to find on sonar. But the USS *Oklahoma* is equipped with our new noise-cancellation system. The sub makes almost no noise underwater. If the captain has decided to stay hidden from us . . ."

"Well, I don't care what it takes," the president demanded. "I want that damned sub found—and found *now!* Do I make myself clear?"

"Yes, sir."

18

"Captain?"

The captain had been dreaming his head was caught in the machinist's vise in his father's home. His father had been tightening the tool; the small head was splitting open. Miller sat in his bunk, realizing that somehow the terrible headache had followed him into his waking life. For a second he was unable to remember where he was.

"Captain?"

Miller got his bearings, then hit the intercom button. "Yes?"

"Sonar, Skipper. I'm getting faint machinery noises."

For a second the captain wondered if his sonar chief was trying to fool him. Then he remembered that the chief was working with him. "How long have we had it with us?" Miller asked.

"Just detected it, sir. But it seems to be shadowing us. It's traveling the same direction and speed we are."

"I'll be there in a minute."

The captain kicked away the thin blanket that had covered him and stood. His uniform was stained and wrinkled. He ran a hand over his bristly chin and then left his stateroom and crossed through the conn.

"Dodd."

"Yes, Skipper?"

"Get the fire-control tracking party working on a torpedo solution for our new friend. Are our torpedoes still ready?"

"Yes, Captain, all four tubes are loaded. We had a fight around tube four. But we got it straightened out. One man's confined to quarters."

The captain swore under his breath as he neared the sonar station. It was the sixth fight since they'd visited Anderson Station. If it hadn't been for the strict military discipline he exercised, Miller was certain many of the sailors would be at each other's throats. It convinced him that there were still spies aboard, agitating the crew, trying to hamstring his operation.

"We're receiving a signal on the gertrude," the officer told the captain when he entered the sonar section of the submarine.

Captain Miller snatched a gertrude phone and held it to his ear. The telephonelike instrument picked up the garbled syllables coming from the submarine following the *Oklahoma*.

"XB6," a watery voice from the sub behind them called.

"They know our call letters," the captain told Dodd, who had just entered the sonar room.

"XB6, you must come to the nearest port immediately," the voice told them.

"That's the third time they've repeated the message," the sonar chief told Miller.

"Tell me if the message changes," the captain told

the sonar officer. "In the meantime can you tell me what we have back there?"

"It's quiet. But definitely one of ours. It nearly matches our computer profile for a Los Angeles-class sub. But I'm not sure which one."

Los Angeles class, Miller thought. That made sense. The Los Angeles-class boats were the most heavily armed submarines deployed by any country. The nuclear-powered submarines carried a huge armament of Tomahawk missiles, UGM-84 Sub-Harpoon missiles, and the standard Mark 48 or newer Mark 50 torpedoes. There was no doubt in Miller's mind that this proved the Soviets were concerned about stopping the *Oklahoma.*

"Dodd, do you have a torpedo situation figured?"

"Yes, Captain."

"Battle stations," the captain ordered.

In a short time the USS *Oklahoma* had swung about to face its pursuer. The *Oklahoma's* noise cancellation system was switched on, making it nearly invisible to passive sonar detection by the American sub it was now facing.

Captain Miller stood in the conn, watching his officers and sailors as they entered data into the fire-control computers. Those working at the machines were double-checked by men using cruder, but effective, paper plots and hand-held calculators.

The captain glanced at the weapons-control panel. It was lit and showed that the torpedoes were nearly ready for launch.

Sonar reported to the captain that the American submarine was in range.

"Flood the torpedo tubes," Captain Miller ordered.

The weapons-control operator checked the display as he went into his torpedo launch sequence.

"Open outer doors," the captain ordered. "How's the solution look?"

"Solution checked and valid, Skipper," the weapons officer said. "Our firing sequence is one, two, three, and four."

"Fire one," the captain ordered in a low voice.

"Fire one."

The *Oklahoma* shivered as an impulse of pressurized air shot the Mark 48 torpedo from the tube, and water rushed in to enter the empty tube.

The Mark 48/Modification 3 torpedo traveled toward the target, a thin wire spindling from it to carry sonar signals back to the *Oklahoma* while relaying any course changes to the torpedo from the sub.

After a quick check of their instruments, the status report was given, "One fired, sir. Functioning normally."

"Cut the wire and fire two," Miller ordered.

Another shudder went through the ship as the second torpedo was sent on its way.

"Two fired and functioning normally."

"Torpedo tube doors closed," another sailor reported.

"Pump out the tubes and reload," the captain ordered.

Far below and ahead of the conn, two teams of sailors struck down torpedoes to load into the empty tubes. They manhandled the green and yellow projectiles, sweating in the close confines of the torpedo flats.

Above, the captain waited impatiently as the sonar man guided the second Mark 48 toward its target. The torpedo traveled only a little faster than the submarine it stalked.

The sonar chief hollered, "They've heard our torp; their screw count's rising—accelerating to full speed, making a hard turn to port." He paused to compensate for the submarine's new bearing. "I have a transient. They've flooded their tanks."

I don't think they can pull it off, Miller thought grimly, feeling sorry for the captain of the other sub. The poor fool was a tool of the communists. Like I was, Miller added to himself.

"Our first torp is off course," sonar reported. "Our second torp's switched to homing sonar. It's approaching their knuckle."

The captain held his breath. The knuckle, the turbulence created when the submarine they stalked accelerated and dived, often confused torpedoes as it bent and reflected the sound waves traveling through the ocean. The captain of the submarine might still manage to escape, Miller thought.

"There goes their noisemaker," the sonar chief reported.

A mistake, Miller thought. They should have set the distraction device off earlier. They must not have expected us to attack, he thought. Or perhaps the captain had panicked and wasn't thinking clearly.

"Torp's through the knuckle," sonar reported. "It's gaining on the sub . . . We got them! We hit the target."

A sound like a distant thunderclap echoed inside the USS *Oklahoma*.

No one cheered. The crew realized that the sailors in the other submarine were Americans, possibly sailors they knew.

Captain Miller grimly plugged into the sonar with his headphones. Though he didn't read underwater sounds nearly as clearly as his sonar chief, he knew what the captain of the other sub would be doing.

Miller and the sonar chief listened as the wounded submarine blew its tanks in an attempt to surface. He waited for the squeal of metal, pushed beyond its strength as internal bulkheads tore away under the pressure of the water around them; that would mark the end of the submarine.

He waited, but the sound never came. The sub is going to make it, he thought. Crippled, but not destroyed. Then there was a faint, secondary sound.

The captain glanced at the sonar officer.

"Torpedo," the sonar officer said, nodding. "Starboard side."

"Left full rudder, all ahead flank," the captain ordered calmly, using the standard tactic of presenting a minimal target to the slow-moving torpedo.

Captain Miller held on to the console as the *Oklahoma* went through its abrupt maneuver.

"Where's the torpedo now?" the captain asked.

"Still pinging. But it's heading away. We lost it . . . No, wait."

The captain stood impatiently.

"We have another one after us. Bearing two-four-six."

"Left full rudder, maintain speed," Captain Miller ordered. The captain of the other submarine was doing just what I would have done, Miller thought. Trying to get even.

"Torpedo bearing two-four-one," sonar called. "This one's pinging on us . . . Third contact bearing two-nine-five. Another torpedo."

As they reached their maximum speed, the *Oklahoma*'s sonar lost its ability to hear anything but the ultrasonic pinging of the torpedoes' active sonar.

"Dive," Miller ordered. "To one hundred meters. Release a noisemaker."

"Full decline on the planes," the diving officer ordered. Then he instructed his men to open the ballast tank.

The knuckle created by the *Oklahoma*'s sudden movement coupled with the noisemaker erected an immense sonic disturbance in the salt water. Would the torpedo racing to catch them be fooled?

Everyone in the conn held his breath.

"It's almost on us," sonar announced. "Wait . . . It's traveling over us. It missed!"

There was a buckling sound as the pressure on the submarine's elastic hull increased.

"The third torp's pinging on us," sonar announced.

Captain Miller crossed to watch over the helmsman's shoulder. The rudder indicator was now amidships, with planes at a ten-degree angle for downward travel. Their speed was thirty-one knots—near maximum for the nuclear-powered vessel.

"She's still coming," sonar warned.

"Five degrees rise on the planes," Captain Miller ordered. "Come left twenty degrees rudder."

"Aye, Captain."

"Release three noisemakers," the captain directed.

"Torp's almost on us," sonar alerted them. He paused for what seemed an endless time to those around him. "It's past!"

"Any more in the water?" Miller asked.

"No, sir. Sounds like the submarine that was following us has surfaced."

"Shall we go after it?" Dodd asked.

"No," the captain said. "They may be damaged, but I have a feeling that sub still has a lot of fight left in it. And I don't care to face any more torpedoes or subrocs. They'll help us if they stay afloat, anyway."

"I don't follow you, sir."

"Well, there's no doubt that they're trying to get us to surrender," the captain said in a low voice. "But ask yourself why. What don't they want us to do?"

"Doc wanted us to surrender."

"And?" the captain persisted.

Dodd gave it a moment's thought. "And he wanted us to believe that Anderson Station had been destroyed by a disease, rather than by some sort of attack."

"Right," the captain agreed. "They even went to great pains to obscure the truth. So it seems to me that there must be something very important in that camp or at least in Antarctica. I'm willing to bet they uncovered a mineral deposit. Oil perhaps. For years everyone's been looking for oil down there without success. I can imagine what the Soviets would do to coerce new oil fields from us. Or to keep us out."

"Perhaps we could interrogate Garrett and Doc," Dodd suggested.

"Maybe." The captain rubbed his temples before speaking. "But she doesn't seem to have it together. First she acts like a complete maniac—now she's a mouse. And we couldn't trust anything we got from Doc. I think we should head for the Antarctic and see for ourselves."

"Our present course is away from—"

"Exactly. I've been traveling away from Anderson in a zigzag course. We'll travel on for a short while longer, then double back. We can still be there in forty-eight hours."

"Captain," the intercom said.

Miller hit the button. "Yes?"

"We've got some more extremely low frequency calls. None with our code, but you asked us to keep you informed."

"Thanks." The captain moved from the intercom. "You know what that is?"

Dodd shook his head.

"They're calling the subs nearest to our position to have them begin a search for us. The Soviets know *we* know about the takeover of the US. They're probably already diverting their subs down here to search for us."

"Yeah, they must be frantic to find us now."

"We're going to have to be really careful. But I think we can do it if we stay alert. And we'll have a few surprises for them when the time comes. Now that crippled sub out there will cause them to assume we're headed northward. While they scramble to block us from reaching Washington, DC, and nuking it, we'll be headed south."

"Sounds good, sir." Dodd nodded.

"All right, then, Mr. Dodd. Have the men plot a new course for the quickest route back to Gould Bay. We have a date to keep in Antarctica."

19

At first Oz had hesitated to take the shot of antibiotic the *Patrick Henry*'s medic had prepared for him. Then he refused it outright and stood to leave the sick bay.

"Look, Captain," O.T. said, looking Oz straight in the eye. "We've been through a lot together. Do this for me. For old times' sake."

Oz glared at his warrant officer as he rolled up his sleeve.

In two hours Oz and Death Song were their old selves, unable to believe their earlier behavior. The ship's medic listened intently to their story of how they felt and what they had encountered at Anderson Station. After a quick consultation with the captain of the *Patrick Henry*, all the sailors who had come into contact with the four Night Stalkers were given antibiotics and all the sailors were alerted to be on the lookout for paranoid behavior among their fellow crew members.

The chief medic made a quick but detailed report of the incident and the ship's captain passed it on to Naval Intelligence.

*   *   *

The next day Oz awoke to learn that the USS *Oklahoma* was missing and the *Patrick Henry* had been ordered to join her sister ship in searching for the missing submarine. The captain of the *Patrick Henry* didn't mince words during the briefing of his officers and Oz: the US *Oklahoma* was to be considered a rogue submarine to be destroyed upon discovery. He went on to tell his stunned staff that the *Oklahoma* had attacked and nearly sunk the submarine that had been shadowing it.

"Gentlemen," the bearded captain of the *Patrick Henry* continued, "while Naval Intelligence believes the submarine is headed northward, our search today will be in deadly earnest. It's possible—especially given the probable mental condition of those aboard her— that she could be headed back into our area. So we need to keep our heads out of our asses during this operation.

"The president himself has ordered that the submarine be destroyed. I can not stress strongly enough that this is a dangerous situation for the entire world. The sub has its full complement of nuclear missiles— sufficient to trigger a nuclear war or turn the major cities of any country into charred piles of rubble. Unfortunately, our Navy is unable to move a fleet into this area in time to capture the submarine. So the duty falls on our heads, and we *are* going to succeed in our mission."

The captain paused, then continued: "If there are no questions, let's get to our search."

Oz's MH-60K had been refitted with its dipping sonar, torpedoes, and sonobuoy dispenser during the sunlit Antarctic night. The chopper was fueled and ready for its crew as the men left the briefing.

The helicopter crew quickly climbed aboard their

aircraft. They were accompanied by naval Lieutenant Ed Buckley, a gangly twenty-two-year-old who would operate the sonar ARR-75XM sonobuoy receiver and launcher as well as the magnetic anomaly detector ASQ-81 dipping sonar, which the MH-60K now carried.

Moments after the MH-60K had lifted from the pad, the naval crew on the *Patrick Henry* wheeled the ship's Seahawk onto the pad and quickly started to unfold its tail and rotors. Once assembled, the Seahawk helicopter would aid in the search for the submarine, sharing its landing pad with Oz's MH-60K by remaining in the air during the periods the Army chopper needed to be serviced.

Oz was again aware of how oddly the MH-60K handled with the torpedoes and sonar equipment. But he found that he was also gradually becoming more accustomed to its peculiarities. At least the controls won't go dead like the ones on the CONCOP, he told himself.

The dark blue ocean raced underneath the MH-60K as it flew into its position; the shadow of the aircraft vanished and reappeared in the rolling waves beneath them. With Death Song's guidance, Oz quickly aligned them into position east of the *Patrick Henry,* which was in line with its sister destroyer, the *Thomas Jefferson.* The Seahawk from the *Thomas Jefferson* flew on the west flank of the ships. The soon-to-be-deployed Seahawk being reassembled on the *Patrick Henry* would take up a position between the two destroyers. This arrangement would enable the two ships and three helicopters to cover a wide swath of the ocean as they traveled toward the last-known position of the USS *Oklahoma.*

*   *   *

"There's a lot of activity up there," Sonar Chief Thomas told the captain of the *Oklahoma.* "Too bad there isn't a wider channel leading back to Gould Bay."

"There isn't," Miller snapped, finding himself irritated with the man's tone of voice. He pointed to the sonar screen. "Those must be the *Patrick Henry* and the *Thomas Jefferson.*"

"Must be," Thomas agreed as he sat at the USS *Oklahoma*'s sonar suite. "It's roughly where they were positioned when we departed from our assigned course." Thomas glanced to one side and snapped a toggle switch. The cramped space around him was crammed with electronic equipment. In front of Thomas was a high gray panel with two large screen displays that fed through the computerized catalog of sonar readings.

As the sonar chief listened with his earphones to the sounds detected by the arrays on the outside of the submarine, the computer tried to assist him in identifying what he heard and displaying the acoustic variables of the ocean around the submarine.

"Yeah," Thomas said. "Two destroyers in the Arleigh Burke class. That's got to be them."

"And they're headed north?" Captain Miller asked.

"Yes, sir. They're coming directly at us. No way we can get around them before they reach us—they're too spread out and traveling at near maximum speed. They're using their active sonar and they have their choppers spread on either side using their dipping sonar." Thomas pointed to a display on his screen.

"They're operating SOP as if they think an enemy submarine might be ready to attack," Dodd suggested.

Captain Miller nodded. The *Oklahoma*'s attack on the submarine that had been trailing them had made the US Navy even more cautious than usual. The two destroyers were on a war footing now, and hunting for the *Oklahoma.*

"Let's see if . . ." the sonar chief started. A tiny light appeared on his screen. "Yes. Right there. That little pinger is another active sonobuoy. They're laying them in a fixed pattern. Must have both helicopters in the air dropping them on either side of the destroyers. There's another. They're all still headed this way."

The captain stared at the sonar display, checked the bathythermograph readout, and then turned and examined the fathometer to determine their depth. "Looks like we have a convergence layer at one hundred ten meters," he said.

"Yes, sir," Thomas agreed. "But it'll just be a matter of time before they start dropping sonobuoys below the layer as well. I'm surprised they haven't already."

The surface water was considerably warmer than the lower strata of cold water. This created an acoustical mirror that would reflect sonar waves upward, making an ideal hiding place for the *Oklahoma,* at least until sonobuoys were dropped below the layer.

"More sonobuoys," the sonar chief warned. "They're continuing to deploy them as they come closer. There's the first one below the layer, sir."

Captain Miller nodded. "Let's see if the next two follow the same spacing and pattern. In the meantime let's take her down slowly below one hundred ten meters. That will protect us from the active sonar on the destroyers at least."

"Aye, aye, Captain," Dodd said.

Moments after the *Oklahoma*'s depth change, Dodd was again standing tensely next to the captain as the next sonobuoys appeared on the screen.

"There's a definite pattern, sir," Sonar Chief Thomas said. "High/low . . . spaced like the others."

"With pretty wide gaps between the buoys," Miller added.

"Probably worried about using up their stocks," Thomas suggested.

"The destroyers are keeping their spacing," Miller said. "Dodd, can you plot a course to take us between the estimated points they'll be covering when they meet us?"

"We'll plot it, Skipper."

"Thomas, keep me posted if anything—anything at all—changes," the captain ordered the sonar chief.

Captain Miller crossed to the attack center. The fire-control tracking party was plotting possible attacks for the two ships approaching the submarine. The pattern of the sonobuoys was even more obvious on the plots; the interval between sonobuoys was two nautical miles—enough for the *Oklahoma* to squeak through with any luck.

"But there's the big IF," Miller said to Dodd, who was studying the plotting as well.

"Pardon?" Dodd asked.

"The question is: how many—if any—passive buoys they're dropping? And if there are some, can we travel quietly enough to pass them without detection? Too bad we can't just sink the two destroyers. But we can't afford to let the Soviets know we've doubled back."

Dodd was quiet.

"Enter your data into the fire-control computers in case we're forced to engage any of the vessels," the captain ordered the fire-control crew. He turned back to Dodd. "Let's go to battle stations," he ordered. "What'd you say, mister?" the captain asked the crewman walking by.

"Nothing, sir," the sailor said in a surly tone.

Miller placed his hand on his pistol and the sailor went on about his duties. The captain had been talking to the men regularly on the intercom, channeling their pent-up fury and trying to keep them in line. To some extent his tactic had worked. But emotions still flared up. One man had been found murdered in his bunk and several were constrained to the gurneys in the sick bay.

For a moment the captain was haunted by the thought that Dr. Pageler was right, that a plague was aboard. But then the captain realized the doctor or some of the spies aboard were poisoning them through the air or water. That had to be the case, Miller thought. Now he would have to push the men and continue as best he could until they had accomplished their mission.

As the submarine went to battle stations, the fire-control team entered data into the fire-control computers; as usual, their figures were double-checked by a second team working with paper plots and calculators. Slowly weapons-control indicators lit up on the panel.

The captain crossed back to the sonar suite. "How's it look, Mr. Thomas?" he asked his sonar chief.

"It's getting murky. The convergence zone is cutting down on the sonar information we're picking up."

"How about our taking a peek above the layer?"

"It'd be a big help."

"How soon before the next drop?" Captain Miller asked his sonar chief. "It's going to be close, isn't it?"

"Real close." Thomas rubbed his aching eyes. "But it should be over the layer. We'll have around ten minutes."

Captain Miller ordered Dodd to take the submarine upward and extend the submarine's sonar mast above the convergence layer for just a few seconds.

As the submarine's mast punched the layer, the sonar board lit up.

"They're staying on the same courses; same patterns," the sonar chief announced.

"Let's head back down," Miller told Dodd.

Before Dodd could give the order to dive below the convergence zone, an angry light appeared on the sonar display.

"Active sonar!" Thomas warned. "From the destroyer—here."

"Classified as Destroyer, Arleigh Burke DDG 51 class," a sonar officer next to Thomas said, reading from the computer identification screen.

"Active sonar's off," Thomas announced.

"They get us?" the captain asked.

"Maybe," Thomas said. "They'll be pinging again any second to check."

"Get us back down, Dodd," the captain ordered.

As the submarine sank below the convergence layer, another blast of active sonar swept the water.

"How about that?" the captain asked, wondering if the *Oklahoma*'s rubber anechoic coating would protect them from detection.

"No, sir," Sonar Officer Thomas answered. "There's no way that could have reflected back. We made it below the layer. They may think they had a false reading on their first sweep. There's their next sono-buoy. It's above the layer, too."

"Let's hang tight then," the captain said. "Maintain depth and speed, Dodd."

"Aye, aye, Skipper."

Captain Miller kept a vigil on the sonar screen, his hands gripping the back of Thomas's chair.

The dots on the sonar screen slowly paced forward as the fleet passed over the *Oklahoma*.

"NS-1, we had a reading directly ahead of you that we'd like you to check," the radioman from the *Patrick Henry* called to Oz. "Turn north forty-five degrees and drop a sonobuoy. You'll be about on top of our last reading."

"Will do," Oz replied, kicking the rudder pedal to bring the MH-60K around. "Got that, Lieutenant Buckley?"

"Yes, sir," Buckley answered on the intercom. "Say when and I'll kick another one out the side door."

"This is NS-1 to *Patrick Henry*," Oz called over the radio. "This the spot we should be in? Over."

"NS-1, you are right on the money."

Lieutenant Buckley pushed a button on his console. From one of the twenty-five slots in the ARR-25XM there was an explosive pop as the pneumatic system fired a sonobuoy from a canister. The tube-shaped buoy rode downward on a small parachute, the debris from the launch tumbling around it. It arched and splashed into the ocean over the *Oklahoma*.

* * *

"Sonobuoy, right on top of us!" Thomas warned as an angry-looking light materialized on the sonar screen, directly over the *Oklahoma*'s position.

"Ahead full speed," the captain immediately ordered. "Right full rudder."

Dodd relayed the order and there was a flurry of activity in the submarine as its engines worked at peak power, propelling the submarine forward at thirty-two knots.

The captain scrutinized the sonar display.

The sonobuoy continued to ping as he watched.

"Patrick Henry," Oz called on the radio. "We have a reading. Repeat, we have a reading on the last sonobuoy. We're transmitting the data to you now, over."

"That's a roger, NS-1. We're copying data coming in from your ARR-75. Hang on . . . Our computers have identified the submarine as an Ohio-class vessel. Since we have no other submarines in this area, it has to be the *Oklahoma.* Prepare to launch your torpedoes on our command."

Death Song armed the two torpedoes on the pylon of the MH-60K. In the passenger compartment behind, Lieutenant Buckley continued to transmit the data he was collecting from the sonobuoy over the ARQ-44 data link that connected them over an encrypted, narrow S-band radio link to the *Patrick Henry.*

"We're losing her," Buckley called to Oz over the intercom. "She's moving fast out of our range."

"NS-1," the radio broke in on Oz's earphones. "They've dropped back below the layer. Drop your dipping sonar and see if you can ping off the sub. We're sending the Seahawks to your sector to help cover the area."

"Roger," Oz answered. "We're dropping our dipping sonar and hovering over the area."

Buckley activated the dipping sonar that swiftly dropped toward the sea on a cable connected to a winch on the MH-60K's pylon.

Captain Miller could imagine what was happening overhead as word spread of the discovery of his submarine. The SH-60B Seahawk LAMPS II ASW helicopters would head for the location to blanket the area where the sub had been detected. The choppers would search with dipping sonar arrays and drop more sonobuoys until they had encircled the *Oklahoma* as she tried to escape from the path the destroyers had taken. And the destroyers and helicopters could match the *Oklahoma*'s speed. There was no way for the submarine to outrun them.

"We're getting increased screw noises on the destroyers," Thomas warned the captain. "They're turning to meet us. Lots of active sonar from their arrays as well. But we're not close enough for those to penetrate the layer now."

The captain turned and crossed to the conn. "Left full rudder," he told Dodd.

"They're setting a new line of sonobuoys," Thomas told the captain as he returned. "They're alternating below and above the layer again."

"Dodd."

"Yes, Skipper."

"Plot a course to take us parallel of the buoys," the captain ordered. He turned back to the sonar display and tapped the screen with his finger. "Those the destroyers?"

"Yes, Skipper." Thomas nodded. "They're going at max speed. But they're following our old course. If we can clear the sonobuoys . . ." his voice trailed off. "Dipping sonar!" he warned abruptly.

The captain saw the sonar on the display screen. "Did they get us?" he inquired anxiously.

"They're still over the old position where the sonobuoy caught us," Thomas answered. "Pretty far away, at the low edge of their detection range. I'm guessing they're not getting a return from us. Looks like they're taking it back to another location." The dipping sonar signature vanished from the screen. "We'll see if they got us on their next drop. If they did, it will be right on top of us."

The captain again gripped the back of Thomas's chair and imagined the helicopter high above them towing the dartlike dipping sonar to its next position.

The seconds ticked by as Miller and the men around him waited tensely.

"There it is again, very faint and much farther away!" Thomas said joyfully. "They didn't get us," he whooped.

The captain left the sonar suite and entered the conn. "Dodd, plot a new course and take us below the closest sonobuoy that's lying above the convergence layer. Let's get out of their sonar net and put some distance between them and us."

"Aye, aye, Skipper."

The captain returned to sonar once more. The dipping sonar had vanished and the screw sounds of the destroyers were fading. The USS *Oklahoma* had managed to escape the destroyers' trap.

20

The Army MH-60K helicopter crew, as well as the naval personnel from the destroyers and helicopters, continued to search for the submarine but failed to get any more definite signals from the *Oklahoma*.

Oz finally returned the MH-60K to the deck of the *Patrick Henry*, where his helicopter was serviced and refueled. While there, he received an order to return to McTavish Station. He was to rejoin the other elements of the Night Stalkers and the Delta Force in order to ferry a group of doctors from the Atlanta Centers for Disease Control to Anderson Station. Once there, the Night Stalkers and Delta Force would protect the doctors, since it was still unclear whether or not an outside attack had been made on Anderson Station.

Oz completed his flight from the *Patrick Henry* to McTavish Station without incident. The brief Antarctic storm of the night before had passed and the air was still as Oz and his men got off the chopper. A distant snowmobile broke the near silence as Oz and his men trudged toward the large geodesic dome of aluminum and plastic that sat in the center of the complex.

Bill Howard, again dressed in his blue parka, plodded toward the helicopter crew. "Ah, Captain Carson. If you'll come this way, I'll take you to the CDC team from Atlanta. They arrived two hours ago. Frank here"—he motioned toward his bearded partner—"can take your men to our canteen."

"I imagine they still remember where it is," Oz said.

"Yeah," O.T. added. "That's one of the key bits of information we always pick up wherever we go."

Howard chuckled as Oz followed him across the ice tarmac. They then stepped onto a path that had been plowed through the snow.

"I hear you're going to check out Anderson Station," Howard said as they approached the large central dome of the complex.

Oz said nothing as they neared the front door.

Howard shoved the heavy metal door. It slid aside smoothly along its roller bearings. The man let Oz enter the airlock leading to the inside of the dome. "I guess I shouldn't be asking about Anderson Station. That's not anything you can talk about, is it?"

"No," Oz replied, removing his sunglasses.

Howard closed the door, sealing out the wind and its noise.

"I'm afraid I'm not at liberty to comment on our mission," Oz explained.

"Things aren't too pretty in here," Howard explained, changing the subject as he opened the inner door. A wave of warm air hit them as they entered the dome.

Oz found himself standing in a large, arenalike chamber whose floor was a haphazard jumble of crates and metal boxes. The confusion spread across the curving expanse of the dome, bathed in the sunlight that streamed through the dome's Plexiglas windows. It was hard for Oz to judge the size of the chamber, but it seemed to him to be at least two hundred meters across.

"It's not pretty, but it's warm," Howard continued as he pulled off his mittens. "Warm's more important than pretty around here any day. If you'll come along with me, I'll show you how to get through this maze."

Howard started weaving a path through the labyrinth of crates.

"Part of the problem is we have to keep our trash and garbage with us so it can be shipped on the cargo planes' return trips," he explained. "Little by little, year after year, we manage to collect more junk than we ship home. Currently, the push is to minimize our environmental impact on the continent. We end up with trash and useless equipment in here and nowhere to put it."

Oz followed the man across the domed stretch until they were nearly under the center of the building. Then Howard turned toward a large boxlike room that was built out of what appeared to be old shipping crates.

"Here we are." He waved Oz toward the archway in the side of the room.

Passing through the entrance, Oz found himself in a room without a ceiling; it was open to admit the sunlight from the dome overhead. A beat-up desk sat on one side of the carpeted room. A worn couch and four folding chairs were arranged in a semicircle in the center of the floor. The two men and one woman who had been seated in the semicircle stood when Oz entered the room.

"Here's your man," Howard told them. "I'll let

you folks get down to business. Let us know if you need anything."

"Thank you, Mr. Howard," a low, husky voice responded.

Oz turned to study the woman who had spoken. She crossed the room and offered her hand. "Captain Carson, I'm glad you're finally here."

Oz found her handshake surprisingly firm. He noted her olive complexion and her eyes, which were so dark they seemed like bronze mirrors. Her sensuous lips, classical nose, and graceful bearing gave her the air of an Egyptian princess.

"I'm Dr. Lee Shahid," the woman said, leading Oz across the room. "This is Dr. Neal Coiner." She motioned to a rake-thin man with an Einstein hairdo and mustache. He waved as he lit up a cigar.

"And this is Lieutenant Lewis Heasty," Shahid continued, and a squat officer in a Navy uniform reached forward to shake Oz's hand.

"Heasty, as you can see by his uniform, is not from the CDC," Shahid explained. "He's going to check the Anderson reactor. There seems to be some doubt as to whether it was shut down correctly. Have you eaten?"

"Yeah," Oz half lied. He had consumed a lukewarm ready-to-eat meal, or MRE, on the helicopter. That was hours before, but he didn't feel hungry and he wanted to get started.

"Good," Dr. Shahid said. "Here's a chair for you."

"Time to pool our ignorance," Coiner said, laughing. Shahid looked daggers at him.

Oz lifted the padded folding chair, scooted it to face Coiner's and Shahid's chairs, and sat down.

"Ten minutes before you arrived," Shahid explained to Oz, "we received a radio message relayed to us from Atlanta CDC. Apparently a vial containing a sample taken from Anderson Station one day before their, uh, emergency had been sent in the return mail leaving the base. It took extra time for the vial to work its way through the system, but it ultimately got to the CDC.

"Our people tested it and found it contained the spores of a very virulent bacteria. It proved to be a heretofore unknown strain of meningococci normally associated with meningitis. The bacteria is readily contracted by the lab animals at the CDC."

Coiner interrupted her, waving his cigar that he held in a stilted manner between his thumb and first finger. "The bacillus starts its attack on the nervous system of lab rats a few hours after exposure. Preliminary tests suggest the contagion would eventually be fatal to human beings, though no work has yet been completed on primates in Atlanta to test this hypothesis."

"The lab animals showed unusual behavior, too," Shahid added, pushing the long dark hair out of her eyes. "The animals often fought among themselves over food."

"Our researchers conjecture that the bacteria might be responsible for the problems at Anderson Station," Coiner continued, gazing directly at Oz as he spoke. "And from what we have heard from the medic at the *Patrick Henry* . . ."

"Yes, definitely paranoid behavior," Oz said, nodding. "And the symptoms vanished just hours after we received the antibiotic."

The room was quiet for a moment. Only the howling of the wind could be heard.

"Just how contagious is this bacteria?" Oz finally asked.

"Very," Coiner said with an inappropriate grin that made his face even more wrinkled than it already was. "Fortunately it's very manageable, as well. The CDC's tests show it has no immunity to penicillin—the medic's prudent treatment of you and your crew bears this out." Coiner sent a puff of smoke toward the open ceiling.

Shahid went on to tell Oz that their task was to make sure the disease was eliminated so it couldn't spread any further. The two doctors from the CDC had brought decontamination equipment and chemicals to treat the base once Oz had ferried them to it.

After she'd finished, Oz spoke: "I don't believe I have any questions."

"That's it then," Shahid said. "How soon can you take us to Anderson Station?"

Oz was aware of her gaze as he checked his watch. "My ground crew will need about an hour to remove some experimental equipment we were carrying. If you can have your equipment there by then, we'll get it loaded onto the pallet for mounting on our cargo hook. We can be on our way ASAP if that's okay with you."

Dr. Shahid held Oz's gaze for a moment and then smiled.

"That sounds very good."

"You three will be riding in the lead chopper with me and the ground crew I'll be taking along, in case we run into mechanical problems." Oz got to his feet. "I'll see you then. I'll be at the canteen briefing the Army personnel under my command if you need me."

21

Dr. Pageler studied Garrett, wondering if she was cured—or merely faking a recovery in an attempt to get him to free her of the constraining straps. The fight with the American submarine had shaken Dr. Pageler. Now he was having trouble trusting his own abilities to make decisions. Got to hang on, he told himself. He knew he might well be the only sane man on board.

Now what about Garrett?

"I feel like I'm waking from a bad dream," she said. "And I'm dying of hunger."

Pageler was struck by how she had the look of a caged bird, with her narrow facial features and thin bones. A bird he was going to set free, he decided without another moment of hesitation.

He loosened the straps holding her arms. "You'll need to take it easy for a bit," he told her. "And you're certainly not up to running any Olympic races. You need to eat a little decent food first."

"What's been happening?" she asked as the doctor helped her to a nearby chair.

"It's a long story," Pageler began, still watching her intently. "The short of it is you—and apparently everyone at Anderson Station—had a sickness that seems to upset the brain's ability to work rationally."

"Then my dreams of people dying— Oh, my God!" Garrett whispered, suddenly very pale. "All those terrible things really happened, didn't they?"

The doctor nodded. "I'm afraid so. You were the only survivor we found at the station." He was quiet a moment and then continued: "Unfortunately, the same thing is happening here on the submarine. Our landing party seems to have caught the plague from our visit to Anderson Station. I've inoculated myself and am trying to convince the captain to protect other key personnel. But I used up most of our antibiotics treating a crewman a week ago, and now there's not enough for everyone—even if the captain were willing to take the situation seriously."

"We have to do something."

"There might be one possibility . . ." Pageler's voice trailed off. He was terrified of his plan. But he knew it was the only way to turn things around on the submarine.

22

Oz quickly explained the new mission—code-named "Grim Reaper"—to the leaders of the three Night Stalkers crews and Lieutenant James Victor, the commander of the platoon of Delta Force troops who would be accompanying them. He explained that they'd be carrying the CDC doctors and the naval nuclear reactor expert to Anderson Station.

"Communications will be poor and resupply will be next to impossible if we run into trouble," he continued, "especially with the storm that is predicted to sweep through the area in the next few days."

"You mean it gets worse around here," one of the pilots cracked.

"That's what they tell me. So we'll have to stay sharp," Oz continued. "We'll have to be on full combat alert since we don't know for certain that Anderson Station wasn't attacked—though that seems unlikely at this time. Any questions?" he asked.

Lieutenant Victor cleared his throat and spoke, "I'm assuming the biological decontamination gear we're packing is because of the communicable illness at the base."

"That's correct," Oz answered. "The submarine crew—and yours truly—contracted a flulike disorder. It can be cured, but it's better to avoid picking it up in the first place. So, while most of our men won't enter the station, those of us who do will need to use C/B equipment—masks, suits, and decontamination gear as the situation warrants it. Be sure your men check their equipment carefully and use it."

"If we run into trouble, can we expect backup?" Lieutenant Eastman queried. "If the station did suffer an attack instead of this sickness . . ."

"We'll have no backup," Oz answered. "We're on our own for all practical purposes. The US is still abiding by treaty regulations from the 1950s, which prohibit a large military presence on the continent. We've been caught unprepared. We're it as far as US representation is concerned in this sector of the Antarctic. Only the Soviets have a military presence; the British, French, and others have no military equipment."

"So we'll have to make our decisions and act on our own if we run into trouble?" Victor asked.

"That's right," Oz replied. "Of course that's not all bad. That means the brass won't be second-guessing us every step of the way."

"Amen to that!" offered Roger Johnson, one of the MH-60K pilots. Several of the men around him nodded knowingly.

"Any more questions?" Oz asked as he paused and studied their faces. "Okay, then. You may brief your men."

Oz's helicopter was in the lead as the Night Stalkers flew toward Anderson Station. Since the Americans were unsure whether the station had actually been attacked, they were taking precautions to remain hidden from radar or visual detection. They flew using their terrain following/terrain avoidance radar that kept them as close to the ground as possible; this would help them remain hidden from radar by obscuring them in ground clutter.

Oz glanced at the environmental control systems panel to his right. The fans were set at their high settings and the temperature control was turned to its top position.

And it's still chilly, the pilot thought. Thank goodness the titanium and fiberglass rotor blades have a heater mat molded into them. Otherwise they'd likely be covered with ice by now.

Behind Oz's helicopter the other three MH-60Ks followed. They bobbed up and down in the same giddy flight pattern the lead helicopter followed. Below each of the choppers was a pallet of supplies or fuel that swayed wildly in the wind and sudden flight changes of the MH-60Ks.

"No radar or radio traffic," Death Song informed Oz. Like the pilot, he had the sun visor of his helmet lowered to reduce the bright glare from the snowy landscape. The navigator glanced at the helicopter's instrument display and noted they were nearing the start point of the route leading to their landing position near the station. "We're nearing the SP," he warned the pilot.

"Okay," Oz said. He triggered on his radio. "Grim Two, Three, and Four, we're nearing the SP. Let's switch from TF/TA to manual."

Oz had them switch from the terrain following/terrain avoidance radar so its faint signal would not give them away as they neared Anderson Station.

Oz disengaged the radar, smoothly taking over control of his helicopter. He dropped the chopper slightly to adhere to a nap-of-the-earth flight they'd been engaged in. The pilot checked the map overlay on his CRT display coming from the mission computer and corrected his course to bring them precisely onto the route they'd selected beforehand.

"Here's the SP," Death Song said after checking the mission control computer on his CRT to be sure it wasn't just another similar peak.

"Silence, silence, silence," Oz ordered over the radio to alert the three pilots behind that radio silence would be observed as they approached.

"Arm our weapons?" Death Song asked.

Oz thought a second. "Yeah. Give me the rockets and the dual MG."

Death Song switched the machine gun controls to Oz.

The pilot watched the terrain ahead of him as he shoved on the collective pitch lever. The craft dropped to retain the radar cover offered by an icy valley.

"Still no radar or radio," Death Song told Oz.

Everything was silent in the cabin except for the whooping of the blades and the noise of the helicopter's twin engines as Oz wove over the terrain. "O.T. and Luger," Oz finally said. "Almost there. Have the Miniguns ready."

The helicopter zipped over yet another rocky hill. Oz glanced at his display. "That the ACP?"

"Yes," Death Song answered after checking the

CRT to be sure it was the air control point landmark. "The RP is coming up."

"Release point coming, O.T., Luger," Oz warned via the intercom.

The pilot pushed forward on the control column, increasing the four main blades' pitch for maximum speed so they would present a fast-moving target should they be headed for trouble. Simultaneously Oz pulled with his left hand on the collective pitch lever, sending the helicopter into the air, over the hill, and abruptly above Anderson Station.

"Anyone see anything?" Oz called as he swung the chopper around in a half circle.

The station they wheeled around was still in disarray as before but now a large drift had formed behind the central dome. Several human bodies were barely discernible in the snow.

"No electronic signals," Death Song said.

"Nothing's moving as far as I can tell," O.T. announced.

"Clear on starboard," Luger added.

Oz triggered his radio, "This is Grim One. Anybody see anything suspicious?"

"Negative," one of the pilots radioed. The others were quiet.

"Grim One, Two, and Three will set down," Oz ordered. "Four, drop off your external sling, then stay in the air with your dogs. Three, your crew will stay in the chopper, ready to relay messages from Four or aid it if we come under attack."

The three pilots signaled that they had heard their orders.

"And everyone remember," Oz continued. "We

need to stay well away from the complex and vehicles until they're decontaminated. Let's use that clearing to the south of the main dome for the landing area."

Oz brought his chopper over the landing position and switched his mike to the intercom circuit. "Let's set our sling down. Can you handle that, O.T.?"

"I've got it," O.T. replied. The crew chief lifted the floor hatch. A blast of cold air greeted him as he gazed through the opening. "Down a meter and a half," he told Oz over the intercom. "Good. Hold it there."

As the helicopter hovered O.T. leaned through the hatch and hit the release knob on the cargo hook. The sling of supplies and decontamination equipment on the hook dropped, lightly landing in the snow below.

"All clear," O.T. said, slamming the hatch and checking to be sure it was secure.

Oz steered to one side of the sling they'd dropped and brought the control column to its center position so they hovered. He pressed on the collective pitch lever with his left hand. The helicopter responded by nearly falling toward the ground. There was a gentle bump absorbed by the hydraulic landing gear and they were down.

"O.T.," Oz said over the intercom. "Be sure to remind our passengers about staying away from the tail rotor. Tell Sergeant Marvin to look over the choppers." The pilot triggered his radio. "Grim Four, this is One. See anything?"

"Nothing but snow and ice."

"Good. Keep your eyes peeled."

"That's a roger, Grim One. Over."

"Grim One over and out."

23

Dr. Pageler nervously fingered the towel he carried, then knocked at the door of the captain's stateroom.

"Who is it?" the captain's tired voice came from inside.

"Lieutenant Pageler. I need to talk to you, Skipper."

"Can't it wait?"

"No, sir, I don't believe so."

There was a pause and a scraping. "Enter."

Pageler unlatched the door and stepped in.

The doctor was startled by Captain Miller's appearance. He was unshaven and his eyes darted around the room. The captain sat behind his desk, which was a clutter of papers, books, and charts. The room smelled of sweat and dirty clothing.

"Captain," Pageler started, "I'm very concerned that this illness we have aboard is endangering the whole crew and ship. We must get to—"

"Damn it, did you come in here to give me more of your nonsense about this stupid head cold," the captain exclaimed.

There was silence as Pageler twisted the corner of the towel he carried.

"I'm onto you, Doc. You know that, don't you?" The captain stood.

Pageler noted the pistol holster strapped to the captain's waist. "I'm not sure I understand, Skipper."

"If you think," the captain continued, "that I'm going to buy that stupid story of yours . . . You thought I'd let you convince me to follow your plans and then get relieved of my command . . ." The man glared at the doctor for a second, then turned his back on Pageler.

As the captain turned away, Pageler let the towel drop to the floor; in his hand he held a hypodermic syringe filled with penicillin. Quickly positioning the instrument in his hand, the doctor lunged toward the captain.

Captain Miller started to turn as Pageler came into contact with him. The needle of the syringe grazed the officer's shirt. Pageler compensated for the captain's movement, grabbing the man's elbow; the needle dug into the officer's muscular arm.

The skipper squirmed away, hitting the doctor's hand before he could push the plunger of the syringe. The needle snapped off in the captain's skin. The officer bellowed in pain and rage.

Pageler stumbled.

The gun in Captain Miller's hand slammed against the doctor's temple. The doctor dropped to his knees, a groan escaping his lips. The syringe fell to the floor, scattering shards of glass and liquid.

A second later Pageler was sprawled on the floor. The captain towered over Pageler, his pistol covering the doctor. The man cautiously probed Pageler's ribs with the toe of his boot.

"Playing dead, huh?" The Captain Miller laughed at the unconscious man. "Well, if that's the way you want it, I'd be happy to oblige you."

The captain pointed his pistol at the doctor, aimed, and pulled the trigger. The explosion echoed down the steel corridor.

Captain Miller holstered his pistol, studying Pageler with satisfaction. He turned and pressed the button of his intercom. "Mr. Dodd?"

"Yes, Skipper?"

"Could you send a couple of men to my quarters? I have a mess that needs to be cleaned up."

"Aye, aye, Captain. Right away."

24

"Do you wish to die in this new Siberia?" Major Churkin Novikov howled as he kicked the soldier who was trudging slowly toward the Mi-6 Hook helicopter that rested on the ice. Novikov snapped off the safety of his short-barreled AKR carbine and motioned menacingly with it at the troops following the laggard.

The major was pleased to see a marked increase in their speed as they jogged toward the chopper.

Stalinist tactics get results, Novikov thought, thinking about the soldier he had killed earlier in the day for failing to get his meal to him on time. That had made an impression on the troops. Now they obeyed him instantly without any of the sluggishness he had come to expect from them. We would have won in Afghanistan if Stalin had been in charge and we'd been allowed to fight more brutally, the major thought.

Despite their fear of him, Novikov felt some of his men were still acting like wimps; they had wanted to stay behind because of their runny noses and aching bodies. The major shook his head. It was hard to believe that these were the grandchildren of the patriots who had brought Germany and Japan to their knees.

It was a good thing he was here to root out traitors and force the others to obey his orders. They would run all over a lesser commander.

Each of the soldiers dashing past wore a snow-camouflage parka, with a hood pulled over a heavy steel helmet that had been painted white with a red star ringed by a laurel wreath emblazoning its front. Most of the men carried an AK74 with its stock folded to fit into the helicopter's cramped interior.

A few of the soldiers entering the chopper carried weapons other than rifles. The sergeants and lieutenants grasped AKR carbines in their mittened hands. Six of the elite troops had BG-15 grenade launchers mounted below their AK rifle barrels; the single-shot launcher was capable of firing a 40mm grenade several hundred meters. A few soldiers carried a bipod-mounted RPK74 machine gun rather than the nearly identical AK74 rifles carried by their comrades.

Each squad also had one soldier who carried an SA-7 antiaircraft rocket launcher. Several other troops carrying rifles also had smaller RPG-18 rockets slung across their backs; these devices were effective against lightly armored ground vehicles, snow tractors, or bunkers.

In addition to their major weapons, each Spetsnaz soldier was armed with a flat-bladed bayonet, RGO fragmentation grenades, and a spring-loaded knife capable of hurling its blade several yards for silent assault of a foe.

As the troops entered the frigid interior of the helicopter, each soldier sat in one of the crude folding chairs in the passenger cabin of the Mi-6 and secured a worn harness around himself.

The ground crew slammed the four side doors shut on the twenty-seven-ton Mi-6 Hook, sealing the two platoons of sixty-five soldiers into the aircraft's belly. All was quiet in the machine except for the thumping of the engine and the arguing of the five-member flight crew as they readied for takeoff.

Novikov had ordered his acre-wide airfield to be carefully plowed only hours before. But despite the inordinate care the crew had taken in clearing the field with the old Russian tractors, the blowing snow was already drifting around the helicopters.

Two members of the Soviet ground crew struggled to get the frozen chocks and chains moved from the giant chopper's wheels. Three other members of the ground crew were struggling to get stiff refueling hoses positioned and the sluggish liquid pumped into the helicopter's tanks, topping them for their long flight.

Major Novikov had hoped to take a third platoon of soldiers on the mission; but the three Hind-Ds that would have carried the men were either broken or refused to start. Now the three machines sat uselessly in the snow; Novikov would have to leave the detachment that would have ridden in them as his reserve. The troops could be transferred into battle only if the Mi-6 Hook came back and picked them up after its first flight—and by then it would be too late for the men to do any good if the battle went against Novikov.

"Have the choppers functional when I get back," Novikov had told the mechanics in charge of maintaining the useless Hind-Ds. "If you fail to do so, I promise you I'll have your hands staked to the ice and you'll be left here to freeze. Now get to work."

Fortunately both Mi-28 Havocs had started, the

major thought to himself as he briskly crossed to the newer of the two gunships. Without the Havocs' firepower, the unarmed Mi-6 Hook would have been defenseless in the air.

The relatively new Mi-28 Havocs were at the base only through a stroke of luck and the major's hard work. Through much string pulling and the calling in of favors that Major Novikov had garnered over his years in Moscow, he had managed to get both helicopters shipped to Soyez III. It had taken the major another full year of skirmishing with bureaucrats to get the weapons pods and ammunition for the two air machines. But now they were assembled, ready to finally be utilized for battle.

Combat preparations and drills for the helicopter crews were nothing new; the major had put them through the drills almost every day since they'd been assigned to Soyez III. But this would be the first time some of them had seen real combat, and for the others, it was the first time since their ignominious retreat from Afghanistan.

But this time it would be different, Major Novikov vowed as he gingerly climbed into his Mi-28 Havoc helicopter, taking care to avoid the five slowly rotating rotors above his head. No agonizingly slow defeat during which Russian soldiers were whittled away by ignorant peasants. This time there would be a quick, decisive victory. This time Novikov would see to it. They would take their objective.

The major settled into the gunner's cockpit, ahead of the pilot, who was already in his own cramped seat above and behind the major. Novikov stowed his AKR carbine beside his cold seat and slid the canopy closed.

He carefully fastened his shoulder harness and then tugged at it to be sure it was secure. Satisfied that it would hold, he turned and studied the other two helicopters nearby.

Their rotors turned gracefully, ignoring the Antarctic wind that hammered against them. Good, Novikov thought. All three were idling properly now that their engines were finally warm.

The major would command three choppers from his attack helicopter as he operated its weapons systems. He was skilled at operating the rockets and machine gun; doing the job himself cut down on the need to convey orders. This way he didn't have to rely on anyone else; engaging in the fighting himself inspired confidence in his men as well.

His plan for taking Anderson Station called for the Mi-6 Hook to land immediately to allow the troops to disembark the vulnerable chopper as rapidly as possible. During this critical moment, his two Mi-28 Havoc gunships would protect the soldiers during the landing, then offer air support to them should they encounter any resistance.

Novikov was not sure there would be any resistance to his attack since there was still no radio traffic coming from Anderson Station. The station was either abandoned, had been devastated (as Dr. Mikhalsky continued to insist), or was a cunning trap laid by the Americans—but Novikov couldn't imagine that the Americans would be wily enough to lay such a trap. That meant the base should be ripe for the picking.

The sun glared off a distant ice face, forcing Novikov to lower the scratched sun visor of his helmet. A few dark clouds to the north hinted at a storm that was moving in from the ocean. But the Soviet commander knew his helicopters would be able to hit the American base before the tempest struck with its clouds of blowing snow.

Major Novikov checked his instruments and then tested the aiming controls for his rockets and turret-mounted 23mm machine gun on the underside of the helicopter. He grasped the fire-control lever, turning it to verify that its servo-motor system was functioning properly.

A TV camera fed the aiming picture into a small screen in front of him as he rotated the machine gun back and forth. A belt of one thousand 23mm cartridges would feed into the gun's bolt when he fired it, giving it the ability to riddle targets on the ground or in the air.

Except for the tendency of the aiming screen for the missiles to fuzz and flicker once in a while, everything was in order in his cockpit. He tapped the screen in an effort to overcome its shorting, then decided its malfunctioning wasn't that critical as long as it didn't become worse. For a brief moment Novikov wondered if American equipment suffered from the same frailties that plagued Soviet equipment.

He plugged the cord from his helmet into the vehicle's intercom. The headset built into his helmet enabled him to communicate with his pilot as well as with the other choppers.

Novikov closed his eyes and took a deep breath, then spoke over the intercom. "Are the preflight checks finished?"

"Yes, Major," his pilot answered. "All three helicopters are ready for takeoff."

Major Novikov punched the helicopters' radio frequency and added it to his intercom net. "One to Two and Three: take off. I'll lead. Two," he told the other Mi-28 Havoc, "you will follow Three."

"Yes, Major."

"Stay low to avoid enemy radar and don't bunch." He signed off so their radio traffic wouldn't attract undue attention if the Americans were monitoring it.

The engines of the three helicopters revved, their rotors increasing in speed with a low-pitched, furious thumping that quickly became a solid drone. Major Novikov's Mi-28 rose from the ice first, looking like an angry insect as it wheeled around the camp below.

Novikov turned in his bucket seat, straining to see if the helicopters behind him were lifting properly. He was satisfied to see the two choppers rise gracefully and fall into position behind him. All three aircraft circled across the bright, frozen plain that stretched before them, then headed toward Anderson Station.

The helicopters flew as low as they dared above the icy troughs and hills that flashed below. The Soviet machines had long since lost their TF/TA radar capability; no one in the Soviet camp had been able to repair the radar because the mechanics didn't have the spare parts. And the spare parts had been on order since the choppers had arrived in the Antarctic.

Oh, well, Major Novikov thought, it can't be helped. The pilots could still avoid the American radar by staying low, at least until the last moment when they were almost on top of the base. Then it would be too late for Anderson Station. The major took solace in the fact that most battles weren't decided by technology but by the cunning and daring of the commanders leading the soldiers.

Soon the three choppers neared their maximum speed of three hundred kilometers an hour, taking advantage of the added lift provided by the thick, cold air they flew in. The major checked his watch.

In just twenty minutes we will be over the American camp, he promised himself. And then it would be Mother Russia's.

25

Oz had grounded all three of the MH-60K helicopters under his command when it became evident that the damage to Anderson Station had been caused by those who had lived, worked, and finally died there rather than by an outside attack. The pilot had ordered Lieutenant Victor to post a few guards around the base, but otherwise the Delta troops were engaged in the cleanup operations at the camp.

Except for a brief flurry of activity when a jumpy guard had mistaken a group of Emperor penguins for a band of men approaching the camp, there had been no sign of danger.

Oz had sent Grim Four back to McTavish base for more fuel and supplies, since it appeared that their work at Anderson Station might take longer than they'd originally planned. He was surprised when the chopper returned not only with a large portable fuel bladder, but two torpedoes mounted on its pylon as well.

He was even more surprised by the new assignment that the pilot of Grim Four hand-delivered to him. Oz was to have the torpedoes ready for use against the USS *Oklahoma* should it return to Gould Bay. The message suggested that the likelihood of the sub returning was slight, but Oz was to serve as the southern end of a net the US Navy was spreading in an attempt to corral the submarine and—if necessary—destroy it. The submarine was still to be considered hostile.

The pilot shook his head. This assignment in Antarctica grew stranger by the hour.

Oz was dismayed, too, at how slowly the decontamination of the station had progressed. It was little wonder they didn't want the bacteria to reach the outside world.

It was also the most grisly task Oz and O.T. had seen since Vietnam.

"At least in 'Nam, the bodies weren't frozen stiff," O.T. remarked, his voice distorted by the black plastic and rubber gas mask he wore. As they walked the two watched the Delta troops who were taking their turn at lugging the dead bodies of the original Anderson Station personnel.

Oz nodded without comment.

The frozen bodies were encased in plastic body bags. Some of the bodies inside were frozen in twisted angles, making them awkward to move and grotesque to view, even under the plastic.

In order to avoid their being covered by drifting snow, the bodies had been stacked by the main dome like cords of firewood. The sight vaguely reminded Oz of photos he'd seen of the bodies piled in Nazi death camps. Human bodies, yet somehow obscenely inanimate, made less than human because of their gruesome fate.

"Let me decontaminate you one more time," Dr.

Coiner told them as he approached. "Then you can remove your masks."

He carefully sprayed them with the contents of an aerosol can he carried. The fire extinguisherlike device bathed Oz and O.T. in a germicidal solution that evaporated almost immediately, chilling them in the process.

"There," Coiner said, his mustache drooping because of the time it had spent inside his gas mask. Unlike the Army personnel, who wore M-40 masks, the doctor had worn a tight-fitting MCU 2-P full face mask, which now hung from a strap around his neck.

"The main dome is uninhabitable," Coiner explained as Oz and O.T. removed their masks. "There's just too much damage. But we completed the decontamination of the dormitory area. By sleeping in two shifts, we can at least have somewhere warm to rest."

"Sounds good to me." O.T. rubbed his chin where the mask had been chafing his skin. "Those inclement weather tents we brought along are for the birds."

"And just between us," Coiner said with a smile, "this old bird about froze its tail off last night.

"Anyway, Lieutenant Heasty has restored the power to that shed over there as well," the doctor continued, pointing to a building straight ahead. "We're setting up our dining area there. We'll still be forced to eat MREs, but at least we can warm them to a decent temperature. And we have running water for showers in the annex to the dormitory."

"Almost like civilization," O.T. snorted.

"And," Coiner went on, "we've erected our lab equipment in that large shed. The rest of the complex is a sorry mess, so we've written it off . . . Ah, Dr. Shahid."

Shahid approached the three men. She wore a white fur coat with knee-high black boots—a marked contrast to the decontamination suit she'd been wearing for almost twenty-four hours. Oz found himself wondering when and how she'd found time to apply her makeup.

"I found the source of the bacteria," she said. "The animal lab was not operational. But someone had apparently opened an old Japanese terror balloon there."

"Terror balloon?" Coiner asked, stamping his feet on the ice to keep warm.

"Yes," Shahid said. "Lieutenant Victor recognized it. Come on, let's get inside—there's room for us in our improvised canteen. I'll tell you on the way."

The four started toward the dome that would serve as their mess hall. Shahid fell in alongside Oz and continued to talk. "How the balloon got here is unknown. But Lieutenant Victor is positive it is from Japan's World War II program. They launched the balloons toward the US mainland. Most were designed to cause forest fires or act as land mines once they arrived."

"I've never heard of such an operation during WWII," O.T. said.

"According to the lieutenant," Shahid replied, "the US Government didn't tell the public about them for fear of creating a panic. And most of the devices were lost at sea before they reached the US anyway. But a few people were killed and it's believed some fires were caused by them."

"But how did the bacteria get into the balloon?" Coiner asked. "We've never encountered this disease in the Orient or anywhere else."

Oz held the door open for Shahid and then entered

the improvised mess area behind her. The domed room still smelled of formaldehyde and alcohol, but was otherwise clean and neat.

"Judging from the number of spores on the balloon," Shahid told them, "the disease wasn't any accident. The Japanese aimed to infect whoever the balloon was being sent to."

"Germ warfare?" Oz asked.

"Exactly," Shahid answered. She unzipped her coat, removed it, and draped it over the back of one of the folding chairs.

The three men pulled up chairs but remained standing as they talked.

"The Japanese experimented with germ warfare," O.T. snapped. "They had a huge complex and they experimented on Chinese prisoners of war—and maybe a few Americans and Brits."

"But why weren't they tried for war crimes?" Coiner protested. "The Germans . . ."

"Because we needed their research for our own germ warfare work," O.T. said. "We gave the head of their program immunity in exchange for his cooperation."

Coiner shook his head and swore.

"At any rate," Shahid remarked, "we now recognize where the disease came from and have contained it at the source. That completes our work here. The catch is the submarine crew that first came here and—in the process—has contracted the disease."

"Right," Coiner agreed. "The submarine is someone else's problem—and a serious one at that."

Oz didn't comment about his new assignment to stop the submarine if it should return. "So your work here is wrapped up?'' he asked instead, unzipping his coat.

"Practically," Shahid agreed, sitting down. "I think you should be able to ferry us back tomorrow sometime if—"

There was a clatter of automatic weapon fire outside. Then Oz heard the thumping of helicopter blades. "Get down," he ordered.

There was another flurry of gunfire; Shahid sat frozen in her chair, unsure what to do.

Oz grabbed her and shoved her to the floor, sheltering her with his body as an explosion rocked the base. Bits of broken glass and plastic fell into the dome.

"You people stay down," Oz ordered Shahid and Coiner as he jumped to his feet. "Get over against the walls where it's safer."

Oz and O.T. drew their pistols and rushed for the door as another blast rocked the complex.

26

The machine-gun firing sent bullets ricocheting off the ice with angry whines in front of Oz as he ran. Oz fired his 9mm Ruger P-85 pistol in the direction of the machine gun, unable to see where it was hidden. O.T. ran behind, blazing away with his Colt Double Eagle .45 automatic.

The two Night Stalkers raced from the dome they'd been in and sprinted across the ice toward their helicopter. Oz was dismayed to see that the fuel bladders, which had been transferred to the base, were blazing. So was one of the MH-60Ks parked at one end of the icy field.

Oz glanced at the Mi-28 Havoc speeding above them. It was completing a missile run toward one of the grounded MH-60K helicopters ahead of the American pilot.

Bullets cracked by Oz as the machine gunner on the ground resumed his attack. Oz swore under his breath as he dashed for his chopper.

"The Americans are fools," Major Novikov muttered, targeting the second MH-60K that waited on the ground next to the base. His chopper swooped through the cloud of smoke rising from the first of the destroyed US choppers. A bullet from one of the American rifles harmlessly splattered on the bulletproof windscreen next to the major's head.

"Two," the major called on his radio to the Mi-6 Hook carrying the ground troops, "get the men on the ground south of the complex. We'll take care of the few American troops firing at us and the last of the helicopters, then we'll mop up on the ground. And remember, I don't want the buildings damaged. There must be something very important in them for the Americans to have this many troops guarding them."

The Mi-6 Hook radioed that it was following the major's instructions.

Major Novikov had the second American chopper in his sights. He ignored the US troops running around the aircraft and centered the targeting screen on the MH-60K itself. He pressed the launch button and then skillfully guided the rocket toward the sitting MH-60K as a pilot clambered into the grounded helicopter.

Novikov's rocket reached the target. A fiery explosion threw bits of the pilot and machine across the ice. The MH-60K's fuel ignited in a smoky fireball that rose above the broken helicopter as the Mi-28 shot harmlessly through it like a moth attracted to a flaming candle.

"Wheel around for another run," Novikov ordered his pilot over the intercom. "We'll get the remaining two choppers on the ground." He switched to his radio frequency. "Two," he called.

"Yes, Major?"

"Get out of my way, comrade! Kill the American

troops that are regrouping opposite our helicopter. You'll be out of my way there. Hurry! I can still take the last two choppers before they can get them into the air."

"Yes, sir." The Mi-28 Havoc swooped to one side to give Novikov a clear run. The Soviet helicopter started strafing the Delta troops running over the ice to meet the Soviets jumping from the Mi-6 Hook that had just landed on the snow.

One thing about the Americans, Novikov thought, they're fast. They'd responded in record time. They had been firing their rifles at the Soviets before Novikov's attack had scarcely been initiated. Now air crews were jumping into the two remaining choppers on the ground and were in the process of starting them. The Soviet major marveled at how well they performed under attack.

My people would still be sitting waiting for orders, he thought as his pilot circled for a final run at the two remaining MH-60Ks.

"But your speed won't do you any good," Novikov said, swinging his machine-gun turret around and peppering the two helicopters below him with bullets as his pilot got into position.

As they started their missile run, Major Novikov abruptly quit firing the machine gun and concentrated on getting his missiles ready for the next attack on the American helicopters.

"Get it started!" Oz yelled to Death Song as the navigator climbed in and shoved the exhausted pistol he'd been firing into his flight vest.

Frantically the two Americans went through only

the steps actually needed to get the MH-60K into the air. Its twin engines refused to turn over in the cold. Oz tried again; for a second the engines failed, then they started their slow rotations.

Oz waited for the engines to come to speed as he plugged the cord from his radio into the intercom. "O.T., Luger?"

"Sir," O.T.'s voice suddenly came on as he snapped the cord on his helmet into the intercom plug. "We're both aboard. One of the choppers's coming in behind us. Looks like it's lining up to launch . . . Missile!"

We almost made it, Oz thought as the rotor reached a high enough rate of revolutions to take off. Bracing himself for the blast of the incoming missile, he lifted the collective pitch lever and they leapt aloft.

But Novikov's missile hadn't been aimed at Oz and his men.

The missile struck the American MH-60K sitting on the ice next to them. The third chopper was blasted apart, its rotors swinging free to clatter across the ice. Bits of plastic and metal wreckage scattered over the white snow and then a shower of flames engulfed the wreckage.

Oz swore loudly into the intercom, unaware that he was speaking. He wheeled his helicopter to the north, momentarily losing the Soviet helicopter that had been behind him. Speeding forward and upward, Oz brought his chopper in behind the other Mi-28 Havoc that was concentrating its fire on the Delta troops below, its pilot apparently unaware of the approaching American MH-60K.

"Can you take that Havoc in front of us with the TOW missile at this range?" Oz asked Death Song.

"It's awfully close," Death Song warned.

"Better take it, we may not have another chance."

"Okay," Death Song agreed. He pulled the controls toward himself and quickly switched them on.

"O.T.," Oz said as he held the helicopter steady for Death Song's shot. "Do you see our other friend?"

"He's coming at us fast but not lined up for attack yet."

"I'm bringing us around," Oz alerted his gunner. "You'll get a clear shot at the chopper on the ground while we take the Havoc in front of us."

"I've got it," O.T. said.

"TOW ready," Death Song announced.

"Fire."

The Mi-28 Havoc pilot in front of the American MH-60K had finally become aware of the American helicopter stalking it. The pilot frantically dropped to the left, trying to avoid the attack he knew must be coming.

The TOW rocket sped from the American chopper toward the diving Mi-28 Havoc. The missile traveled on a tail of fire as Oz held his helicopter steady. At the same moment staccato bursts from O.T.'s Minigun created a din from the rear of the MH-60K as he fired at the Soviet troop carrier below.

The Soviet helicopter ahead of Oz avoided the TOW for a moment. Then Death Song centered the Mi-28 Havoc on his screen. With only a fraction of a second to spare, the missile dropped and struck the helicopter.

The Havoc tore apart as the TOW rocket collided

with its engine. The helicopter didn't explode. Instead, the giant rotors came loose, crashing through the fuselage and ripping off the machine's tail. The machine was instantly unable to sustain its flight. It plunged to the earth, shattering like a child's toy on the ice below.

"The other Havoc's coming in from the left!" O.T. warned. "At five o'clock." He fired a long burst toward the incoming helicopter. "Missile launch!"

Oz threw the helicopter to the right in a steep bank that nearly rammed them into the low hill of snow that seemed to come speeding toward them. For a terrible moment Oz wondered if O.T. and Luger had fastened their safety harnesses. If they hadn't, chances were good they'd be out of action.

The Soviet missile steamed toward the American helicopter, ignoring the flare that Death Song released from the countermeasures pod. Then the guided missile raced past, barely missing the MH-60K and striking in the valley ahead of the Americans, showering their chopper with bits of metal. The metal shrapnel was stopped by the chopper's thick windscreen and skin as the Americans darted through the plume of snow, ice, and metal.

"He's still on our tail," O.T. warned, nearly freezing as he stuck his head out the gunner's door to peer behind the helicopter. "He's coming down to pick us up again."

Oz shoved forward on the control column, increasing the four main blades' pitch for maximum speed. Simultaneously the pilot used his left hand to pull on the collective pitch lever, lifting the helicopter into a steep climb that threw him backward into his seat.

Like other MH-60K helicopters, it was impossible

for the one Oz flew to complete a loop. But in the heavy
Antarctic air, Oz came as close to a loop as he could
in his frantic effort to escape the Mi-28 Havoc that was
dogging them.

The pursuing Soviet helicopter fired a brief burst
from its machine gun that tore into the rear of the MH-
60K. The metal fragment indicators lit in front of Oz
as he continued his precipitous ascent.

And then the Americans were out of the Mi-28
Havoc's sights.

Behind them, Major Novikov cursed his pilot for
not anticipating the American pilot's maneuver, then
he cursed Soviet technology for not being able to match
that of the US.

That American pilot's good, Novikov thought as
his pilot forced the chopper into a steep climb and
turned in an effort to keep the MH-60K from getting
behind them.

A stream of fire from the Miniguns on the side of
the MH-60K smacked against the Mi-28 in front of Novikov's cockpit. The .30-caliber bullets spaulded the
front windscreen and several warning lights blinked to
life on the panel in front of him. The major was aware
of a stinging cut left on his cheek by a glass fragment.
The shooting stopped as the Americans turned away
from the Mi-28.

They're good, Novikov thought. In just a few minutes they had not only escaped his attack, but had even
managed to destroy his other Havoc. And the American chopper's machine-gun fire seemed to have crippled the Mi-6 Hook on the ground as well; Novikov
looked downward where his troop carrier now sat life-

lessly on the ground as the Soviet troops scattered from it.

One American helicopter had nearly wrecked his plans!

Novikov swore at the strangers in the aircraft. They were good, but he would see to it that they would pay for what they'd done. This he vowed as they circled to face the MH-60K.

27

Lieutenant Victor, the leader of the Delta Team at Anderson Station, ignored the helicopters above him as he dropped to one knee. Another burst of bullets glanced off the ice-crusted snow where he'd been, splattering bits of cold grit all over him.

The American soldier caught his breath. He knew Oz had given them a fighting chance when he'd downed the Soviet chopper. The Spetsnaz troops had been cutting his men to ribbons, but now the Americans had a ghost of a chance of defending the station.

Victor saw the flicker of movement in his peripheral vision. He whirled, mashing the trigger of his carbine.

The giant Spetsnaz soldier leapt over the drifted snow, his AK74 raised to fire. Victor's burst caught him first. Bloody holes riveted the soldier's white snowsuit as he tried to aim his own rifle; his finger clasped the trigger, sending flames into the snow at his feet as he fell.

A more cautious comrade behind the fallen Russian peeped over the drift.

Victor swung his rifle downward and fired another

stream of slugs that stitched into the drift, catching the Soviet in the chest and throat as he tried to hide behind the fluffy snow.

A third soldier jumped the drift, his gun blazing as he fired wildly, unsure where the American who had shot his comrades was.

The Soviet's shot went wide of Victor, but smashed into the face of the Delta private that came running up behind the American. The .22-caliber slug tore through the private's ballistic helmet and into his brain. He crumpled, the momentum of his running causing him to roll forward into a limp pile beside the lieutenant.

Victor tapped his carbine's trigger before the Soviet soldier could recover from the recoil of his own shot. The Soviet soldier attempted to wade through the drift and the M16's slugs caught him in the chest. He sprawled onto the ice at Victor's feet.

The American lieutenant crept toward the drift and carefully glanced over it. Perhaps fifty meters in front of him, five Spetsnaz troops were charging toward him. The American took careful aim and fired a salvo of bursts, his finger pumping the trigger of his carbine.

The bullets cracked among the men. One dropped to his knees as Victor continued to mash his trigger. The five grasped at the wounds on their bodies as they fell in a tangle of limbs and weapons.

Releasing the empty magazine from his smoking carbine, Lieutenant Victor turned to see a group of his own men racing through the snow toward him. He shoved a full magazine into his weapon and slapped the bolt release so the carrier slammed forward, chambering a round.

"Their chopper landed over there," he said, gesturing with his mittened hand toward the Soviet helicopter. "We need to cut them off from the base. Jones."

"Yes, Lieutenant."

"I want you to get to our men pinned over there," Lieutenant Victor said, pointing. "Get them organized to initiate a flanking maneuver from that side. I'm going to get the rest of us lined up to guard the buildings around the main dome. Got that?"

"Yes, sir. Flanking movement from that side."

"Wait a minute," Victor ordered, pulling a smoke grenade from his pocket and ripping out its pin. He tossed it toward the open area in front of him. After several seconds a white cloud of smoke started pouring from the grenade.

"We'll provide cover," Victor shouted to Jones, "now go!" The lieutenant and his men stood, shouldered their rifles, and fired toward the Soviet troops they knew must be on the other side of the smoke.

With the fire helping to provide cover, the private ran across the smoke-covered open stretch between the two groups of American soldiers. Lieutenant Victor ordered a cease fire as soon as Jones reached his new position. The Americans dropped to the snow as a salvo from the Soviet side answered their own.

After the flurry of shooting had ceased, Victor again rose to one knee. Through the smoke, he could barely discern the shadowy shape of another Spetsnaz soldier, peering through the smoke trying to see what was going on as he crept forward.

Victor centered the aiming dot of his Aimpoint scope on the Soviet and squeezed the trigger. His carbine sent a burst of bullets to stitch the form of his adversary, who dropped to the ice.

All was quiet for a moment except for the low moaning of the Soviets lying on the icy plain in front of Victor. Then he heard the scrunching of boots in the snow behind him. He swung around, his rifle ready. He was relieved to see the rest of a squad of his own Delta troops charging forward to join the troops spread around Victor.

The ten men spread as they dropped into the snow beside the lieutenant and the five others. An RPK74 machine gun thundered from the ice hill opposite them. Despite the screen of smoke that covered them, the Soviet's aim was nearly perfect. The snow around Victor was penetrated by slugs, and the soldier next to him cried out and went suddenly limp.

The lieutenant ignored the sudden burning in his leg as he peered through the dissipating smoke. The Soviet machine gun fired another blast that sent bullets cracking over the Americans.

Victor knew the RPK74 was behind the ice hill. But he tried to pinpoint it before returning fire. For a moment Victor couldn't see the gunner. Then he spotted the man's face and rifle, silhouetted against the white snow around him. Victor took careful aim and squeezed his trigger. Abruptly the Soviet weapon stopped firing as the machine gunner dropped from sight.

Victor turned back to the men around him. "Okay," he said loudly so everyone could hear over the din of the sporadic firing. "We need to spread along this perimeter of the station. Your job is to protect it from the forces advancing from the cargo chopper that landed north of us. Now go!"

The soldiers spread to either side of Lieutenant

Victor. "You stay next to me," he ordered the Minimi gunner who was starting to leave.

The machine gunner lay prone beside the lieutenant and planted the bipod of the Minimi so the gun lay to the side of the drift the two men were hidden behind.

The Spetsnaz troops started their assault before the Delta troops had time to completely spread along the line the lieutenant had tried to create. The Soviet commandos charged over the snowy hill, their weapons blazing as they advanced.

The Minimi gunner next to Victor opened up with his weapon, skillfully firing short bursts at the exposed Soviets dashing down the hill. Victor added his fire to that of those around him, taking careful aim to conserve his dwindling ammunition.

Ahead of the American line, Soviet soldiers were falling.

Victor shot one combatant and then took careful aim at another. The soldier fumbled with a BG-15 grenade launcher and then dropped to one knee to aim it.

Victor scoped the grenader and squeezed the trigger. The man with the BG-15 staggered, spinning about to expose a bloody stain on the back of his white coat. He dropped, then rolled down the hill.

Victor glanced back toward the dome.

There were no enemy troops there yet. But what he saw was nearly as surprising. Dr. Shahid was running toward the American line, an M16 rifle snatched from one of the fallen Delta soldiers grasped in her arms.

What is she trying to do? the lieutenant asked himself. He swore under his breath as he turned back toward the enemy.

The Soviet assault seemed to be petering out. Only

two men were still running toward the American line. There was a brief flurry of shooting among the Delta troops and the Russians were lying dead in the snow.

"Hold your fire!" Victor called. He turned to Shahid who knelt in the snow beside him. "What the hell are you doing here?"

"What's it look like?" she asked, jerking back the charging handle on her rifle and letting it clatter forward to chamber a cartridge. "You think only men can shoot rifles?"

Victor ignored her question as he scanned up and down his line. Several of his soldiers had been wounded, but most were still alive and in position to repel another assault.

What's happened to our flanking movement? Victor wondered.

He was suddenly distracted by the twin thumpings of two helicopters reapproaching the base. He glanced upward as the dogfight began.

28

Oz took his helicopter in an ever higher spiral as he and the Soviet Mi-28 Havoc fought to gain altitude on the other while avoiding each other's guns and rockets.

"Stay ready with the TOW," Oz told Death Song. The pilot switched to the frequency for McTavish and pressed the trigger on his control column, activating the radio.

"Grim One calling McTavish, come in please, over."

There was no answer. He repeated his message several times as he fought to keep his chopper above the Mi-28 Havoc below him.

There was a torrent of static and the radioman at McTavish answered. "We're copying, Grim One, go ahead."

"Anderson Station is under attack, repeat, under attack, over," Oz told the radio operator at McTavish.

"We copy, Grim One. What are you facing, over."

"Three Soviet choppers—one's still in the air and on our tail—and a fifty- or sixty-member contingent of ground troops. They've destroyed three of our choppers and our fuel depot. Request air and troop support immediately, over."

"That's a negative, Grim One. We have no military planes here at McTavish. The storm moving your way has locked in the choppers to the nearest bases south of your position, over."

"How long before we can expect backup, over."

"Days at the soonest . . . You guys are just on the edge of the storm. But our main bases are going to be buried in blowing snow—and they weren't prepared since the storm has developed unexpectedly. Sorry, over."

"We'll get back to you, McTavish. Right now we've got a Havoc to take care of, over."

"Roger that, Grim One. Good luck, over and out."

Oz had managed to remain above the Mi-28 Havoc, but the Soviet pilot was still on his tail. This made it impossible for either chopper to get a clear shot at the other.

"We're losing fuel fast," Death Song warned. "We seem to have developed a leak in our tanks."

"I wouldn't doubt it," Oz said, recalling the salvo the Havoc had hit them with. Even self-sealing tanks like those of the MH-60K had their limits.

"I think I could at least harass him if you took us into a tight turn," O.T. suggested over the intercom.

"Let's try it," Oz told him. "I thought we could outlast him until he ran out of fuel and then take him. But it looks like we'll be empty first. Ready, O.T."

O.T. set his Minigun for continuous fire rather than ten-round burst so he could do maximum damage if he should be able to get a shot at the Soviet aircraft glued to their tail.

"Ready and waiting," the warrant officer answered.

"Here we go." Oz shoved the control column to the left as he kicked the left rudder pedal, causing the helicopter to go into a tight turn as they continued to rise.

The pilot of the Mi-28 Havoc was momentarily taken off guard. Before he could react, he was exposed in O.T.'s sights.

O.T. squeezed the trigger.

The Minigun screamed a burst of rapid fire, cartridges and links raining from its shoots as a stream of flame and bullets raced from the weapon's six rotating barrels.

Major Novikov had been raging at his inability to fire on the American helicopter above them. Like his pilot, he was surprised by the sudden turn the MH-60K made. He was aware of the fiery blast from the American helicopter's Minigun; a fraction of a second later, the bullets thumped into the Mi-28, cutting into its starboard pylon, ripping one of its rockets from the mountings, and setting off alarms in Novikov's cockpit.

The stream continued, stitching into the fuselage above the major, cutting across the pilot's cockpit, spaulding the windscreen, and throwing glass fragments into the pilot's face.

Though the pilot's eyes were protected by his helmet's sun visor, the gashes in his face and neck were deep and painful. He was alarmed to see blood spurting from a neck wound. The blood seemed to jet, covering his controls and blotting the instrument dial in front of him.

Reflexively the Soviet pilot jerked his control column to the right, kicking the right pedal at the same time. The Mi-28 Havoc rolled away from the Americans, escaping the murderous hail of bullets.

"No! Go after them!" Novikov screamed into the intercom.

There was no reply and the Mi-28 started to whirl out of control.

"What's wrong?" Novikov bellowed. Frantically he grabbed the dual column control in his cockpit, taking over for the apparently unconscious pilot.

"Are you badly hurt?" the major called over the intercom, jerking on the stick.

There was still no reply from the dead pilot of the Mi-28 Havoc.

"He was rolling clockwise and dropped from sight behind us," O.T. informed Oz. "He seemed to be heading away from us. I got a long burst on them but I don't think I did any real damage unless we just happened to get lucky. I'm also out of ammunition."

"Whatever you did," Oz said, "you got him off our tail. That's what counts. Death Song, let's see if we can find him for a clear shot." Oz continued the tight spiral, bringing them around to face where the Mi-28 Havoc should have been.

"Anybody see him?" Oz asked. Unlike the MH-60K, which was painted dark black, the Soviet chopper had been painted white to blend into its snowy surroundings. Now it was proving nearly impossible to see.

"He's dropped off radar," Death Song said. "He must be in the ground clutter. And we're almost out of fuel."

Major Novikov circled his helicopter away from the MH-60K, dropping as fast as he dared toward the ice below. The major could fly the helicopter, but he knew the limits of his skills. He understood there was no way he could face the American chopper and prevail without a skilled pilot backing him up. And right now, he knew his skilled pilot was either unconscious or dead. The Soviet major decided it was time for him to retreat to Soyez III and collect a new pilot and—if his mechanics had done their jobs—the Hind-D helicopters.

In the meantime, he assured himself, my troops at Anderson Station should be able to take the base without me—if they were going to in the first place.

Novikov kept the chopper as close to the ice as he could safely fly and checked the compass so he could adopt a direct path toward Soyez III. He glanced at the storm cloud that was almost on top of him and wondered if he had time to reach Soyez III before the tempest swept over the entire area.

"Could he have crashed or landed?" Oz asked, searching below them for any sign of the Soviet Mi-28 Havoc.

"I still don't think he was hurt that bad," O.T. answered. "And I sure don't see any smoke or wreckage."

"There he is!" Luger hollered. "Low at two o'clock."

"I see him," Oz said, turning his chopper so it was

headed at the Mi-28 Havoc. "He's traveling full out. Death Song, do we have enough fuel to overtake him?"

"No way. We need to land. *Now.* We're running on fumes."

"How about a quick shot with the TOW? The Havoc's still in range, isn't it?"

"He's still well within the four-thousand-meter range. But the Havoc's traveling at its max speed. It'll be touch and go—even if we stay in the air."

"Let's try."

Death Song had been ready with the missile's joystick controls and monitor extended in front of him. With Oz's order, the copilot initiated the launch of the TOW. The rocket streaked from its tube, its eight fins popping into place in a blur of motion as it reached its maximum speed of slightly over one thousand kilometers per hour.

"We've got rocket launches from the ground!" Luger warned. "Low at four o'clock, near the transport helicopter."

Oz glanced from his side door and saw the telltale smoke trail that marked a rocket launch. It was far away, but still a concern. The rocket exhaust showed that the aim was off; Oz held the helicopter steady for Death Song as the warhead burst two hundred yards away.

"Larger rocket!" Luger warned.

Oz had seen the rocket a moment before Luger shouted the warning. He instantly jerked the helicopter to the left, placing the chopper into an evasive dive.

Death Song swore as he lost the Mi-28 Havoc in front of him. He released the joystick as the TOW wandered from its target, veering under the Soviet helicopter and exploding in the ice.

As the MH-60K fell to the side, Death Song reached to release a flare from the countermeasures pod; the brightly burning object shot through the air behind them.

The heat-seeking SA-7 missile behind them streaked toward the hot flare. It exploded twenty meters behind the MH-60K.

"Close," Oz sighed after the loud clap had passed them.

A beeping accompanied by flashing light on the panel in front of Oz signaled that the helicopter's tanks were completely empty of fuel. "Secure your Miniguns back there," he warned O.T. and Luger. "We're out of fuel. I'm going to have to gyrocoast us in."

The blades of the MH-60K automatically assumed their optimum pitch, disengaging from the engine as it exhausted its fuel. The rotors then acted somewhat like a parachute to slow the descent of the chopper. The cold air whistled past the skin of the suddenly silent helicopter.

29

While the landing would be rough, Oz knew the hydraulic system on the three landing wheels would absorb much of the shock. The chance of landing with only minor damage to the chopper and none to the crew was quite good.

The pilot's major concern was the Mi-28 Havoc and the Soviet ground forces. Would the Soviets be able to take advantage of the American chopper's inability to maneuver?

"O.T., did you say you were out of ammunition?" Oz asked.

"Roger that," O.T. replied.

"Luger?"

"About five hundred rounds left."

"I'm going to fight the controls and try to take us over the base. Set your gun on ten-round bursts and see if you can take out those rockets around the grounded Hook. Then take targets of opportunity. Let's give the Delta troops a last few minutes of air cover."

"Will do," Luger said with a grin. The idea of going down with weapons blazing appealed to the young gunner.

The American chopper dropped at an alarming rate. Oz carefully guided it toward Anderson Station, taking care to place his right side toward the Soviet lines so Luger could have a clear field of fire. The pilot lifted the sun visor on his helmet so he could see better in the darkness that had been brought on by the thick storm clouds.

As the helicopter neared the ground, Luger carefully aimed his Minigun, firing ten-round bursts at any target he could find. He pumped the controls of his weapon until his fingers hurt, saturating with fire enemy soldiers who were frantically trying to get a malfunctioning rocket to launch at the chopper.

Luger then concentrated on a line of Soviet soldiers attempting to counterflank the Delta troops. The deadly rain from the Minigun cut the enemy soldiers apart. Luger squinted into the snow that was starting to sweep into his window as the storm finally fell over the base.

He pulled the trigger on the spade grips of his weapon once more and was rewarded with a final burst. Then his weapon was empty.

"Hang on!" Oz warned.

Luger secured his weapon. Its barrels sizzled as ice blown by the wind settled on them and quickly turned to steam.

Oz fought the chopper's rotors in an effort to avoid a bank of ice, and then the MH-60K slammed into the snow north of Anderson Station with a bone-jarring slap.

Death Song sat stunned for a moment in his bucket seat.

"Come on!" Oz hollered at him, shaking his shoulder in an attempt to bring the navigator to his senses. "We need to defend ourselves. There're ground troops headed our way."

"Uh . . . Okay," Death Song answered, unbuckling his harness. He turned and snatched the Steyr AUG rifle from behind his seat.

When Oz saw that Death Song was all right, he quickly spoke into the intercom, "O.T., Luger, you okay? We have enemy troops coming from three o'clock."

"We'll exit the left side door," O.T. answered.

Oz snatched his PK-15 stockless carbine from behind his seat, made sure that the forty-five-round Thermold magazine was latched in place, and cycled the charging handle, chambering a cartridge into the weapon. That done, he leapt from his side door, staying low to avoid the volley of shots that bounced off the ice in front of him.

The pilot scrambled through the deep snow that refused to support his weight and dropped to one knee behind the bulletproof shelter offered by the aircraft. Another burst of bullets glanced off the ice-crusted snow and thumped against the nose of the helicopter. Oz ignored the danger as he raised his gun and took careful aim at the charging soldiers.

He triggered a three-round burst and was satisfied to see one of the Soviets nearly one hundred meters away stumble and fall.

"How many are out there?" O.T. yelled, firing off a flurry of shots as he knelt next to Oz.

"We've got ten or fifteen charging us from there." Oz pointed with his gun. He paused to fire another volley. "I'd be willing to bet they're headed in from another direction as well." He turned to search for Death Song and Luger, then saw them on the snowy hill beyond the tail of the MH-60K. Luger fired a burst from his Calico 950M stockless carbine. The empty 9mm cartridges spewed from the ejection port at the bottom of his short weapon.

"Looks like Death Song and Luger have us covered," Oz told O.T. between bursts of fire. Oz turned back to the advancing enemy troops. "You take the ones on the left and I'll concentrate on the right. Better take it easy on the ammunition. I dropped us behind the Soviet line." Both men knew that once they depleted their ammunition, they'd be out of luck.

The Spetsnaz troops regrouped for another charge at the American helicopter. Oz jerked the trigger of his PK-15 carbine repeatedly. Many of his shots went wide; there was no longer time to aim carefully as the enemy soldiers narrowed the space between them and the helicopter with their onslaught.

Eight Spetsnaz soldiers came with their AK74 rifles blazing on full automatic. They, too, were unable to aim. Rather, they threw slugs in wide patterns that left the air around Oz and O.T. crisscrossed with tracer paths and the cracks of the supersonic bullets.

One of the Spetsnaz triggered a grenade launcher; the weapon made a blooping report, and then the shell exploded harmlessly behind Oz.

Oz discharged his PK-15 again, knocking down the soldier with the grenade launcher as he struggled in the open to insert another shell into his weapon. At the same moment O.T. fired a burst from his advanced combat rifle. His salvo caught one of the soldiers in the face, smashing the man's forehead and ski goggles.

The sound of bullets thumping into the MH-60K above their heads made the two Americans duck for a moment. Oz jerked his nearly empty magazine from his PK-15 and snapped his last magazine into it. He glanced at his now-empty magazine pouch, took a deep breath, and raised his weapon and head, braving the flurry of bullets passing through the air around him.

O.T. bobbed up with him and the two men's guns blazed at the charging Soviets, cutting down the five who remained.

"Here come more!" O.T. yelled, pointing to the west with his gun barrel. The warrant officer swore as he noted the open bolt on his gun. "And I'm out of ammunition."

"I'm on my last magazine," Oz admitted. "Check with Death Song, he may have some cartridges left in his M9 pistol."

O.T. scampered up the hill toward Death Song and Luger, who continued to fire at distant targets.

"Got to make it count," Oz told himself as he fired only one shot per trigger pull in the semiauto mode. He peered around the nose of the helicopter, resting his weapon against the aircraft to steady it. He took careful aim, barely able to see in the snow and ice blowing across the drifting field. He squeezed off seven aimed shots.

Five of the enemy soldiers fell to the snow.

Without warning there was a riot of gunfire to Oz's side.

Oz swung around to see four more Soviets running around the front of the chopper, now nearly on top of him. Unconsciously he thumbed the selector of his weapon back to its three-round burst position.

Bedlam erupted around Oz as he pumped the trigger on his gun, aiming by instinct rather than by using his weapon's Aimpoint sight. Three of the Spetsnaz soldiers tumbled at his feet. He pulled the trigger as he aimed his PK-15 at the fourth. The hammer was locked back by the open bolt carrier. His gun was empty.

Oz dodged the razor-sharp bayonet the charging soldier jabbed at him. Then the American pilot smashed his empty gun barrel into the Spetsnaz trooper's face, shattering the soldier's nose and knocking him unconscious.

Oz whirled toward the remaining Soviet soldier who stood motionless, his eyes wide. The giant trooper seemed frozen in place. Then a trickle of blood dropped from the corner of his mouth and he dropped his rifle.

"Got him," O.T. said between clenched teeth, appearing from behind the Spetsnaz trooper. O.T. jerked his Bowie knife from the soldier's back as the Russian fell at their feet.

"They're all out of ammunition, too," O.T. announced grimly, gesturing toward Luger and Death Song, who were advancing toward the helicopter.

There was a flurry of shots on the field beyond the helicopter as Death Song and Luger joined Oz and O.T. at the nose of the helicopter. O.T. picked up the Soviet rifle lying in the snow and then threw it down when he found it was empty. Oz decided to use his empty carbine as a club; the other three Americans beside him held their battle knives ready.

For a few seconds there was only the howling wind

and the stinging snow and ice of the storm. Then they heard the noise of boots approaching on the other side of the chopper.

Suddenly a soldier in a white snowsuit pounced around the nose of the helicopter, his rifle pointed at the four Night Stalkers.

30

Grace Garrett sat in a state of shock in the *Oklahoma*'s mess hall. Everyone she had known at Anderson Station was dead. Then Dr. Pageler . . . And now other members of the submarine were getting sick and dying, too. Only the captain's iron-clad discipline and his ability to harness the crew's hatred and fears and focus them on the Americans trying to stop the submarine kept the crew from fighting among themselves. But that couldn't last. Garrett was sure the killing would start again and there was nothing she could do to stop it.

She poked at her mashed potatoes, then shoved the tray away from her.

As usual, no one came close to her. They treated her like a leper.

The captain had given her limited access to only a few parts of the sub, but she was a virtual prisoner in the *Oklahoma*. And she was concerned about her physical safety on a submarine full of unstable sailors.

"Excuse me," a lanky black man said as he leaned over the empty table. He glanced to the side to see if anyone was watching. Satisfied no one was observing them, he half hid his mouth with a bandaged hand as he spoke. "The crew's going crazy, isn't it? Just like they did at your base."

Garrett said nothing.

"Isn't it?" he repeated.

She nodded.

"Well, I need to talk to you. We can't sit around and let it happen. I want to know what's wrong . . . I'll be waiting in the corridor. If no one is following you, we'll talk."

He was gone before she could reply.

Was he sane? Garrett wondered. Or was he acting out his own paranoid delusions, thinking the rest of his companions were mad and he wasn't? Or did it make a difference?

She stood and plodded to the conveyer belt that lugged the empty trays toward the galley. Turning, she passed two crewmen arguing about who the best president of the US had been; she left the mess hall.

The corridor was empty. She walked toward the passage leading to the tiny room the captain had assigned to her.

"Here," a whisper sounded beside her.

She started at the unexpected sound and noticed a hatchway that was open only a crack. It opened wider to expose the face of the black man who had spoken to her in the mess. "In here."

Garrett hesitated, then stepped over the lip of the hatchway.

"We don't have much time," the black man whispered in the dimly lit chamber. Garrett read his name, Post, from his uniform pocket.

"The captain killed the doc," Post continued. "I overheard them discussing how the crew would go crazy like the people did at Anderson. You were crazy—but now you're sane. What's happening? Did Doc cure you?''

"The disease that we had at Anderson," Garrett explained, groping for words, "it's contagious—but Dr. Pageler discovered he could cure me with penicillin. He wanted the captain and officers to have shots of the antibiotic and then take the sub to the closest port to get more. Dr. Pageler said he'd expended most of the ship's stores during a recent accident."

"Ahhh," Post exclaimed, raising his bandaged hand. "That explains it, then. I'm the guy he pumped the penicillin into. I got cut real bad when I was working inside a control panel and he sewed me up and loaded me full of penicillin. That's what's kept me from going crazy like the rest. Damn."

"We've got to escape."

"Lady, unless they fire you from a torpedo tube, there's no way you're going to get outta here!"

"Then a message, perhaps. If the authorities knew what was happening . . .''

"I sent a message from Doc when we first brought you aboard," Post said. "I'm senior radio officer. They know we're catching what you had at Anderson. And by now the Navy knows we've gone rogue. All they have to do is put two and two together—something they can do real well when a sub full of nuclear missiles comes up missing. The catch is, they have no way of knowing where we are."

"Could you send a message?"

"That's what I'm going to try to do when we surface. But it's risky as all get out. They'll kill me for sure if I get caught. Hell, the captain already thinks we have communist spies aboard. He'd probably shoot us both if he caught us here. But we've got to—"

The hatch swung open suddenly.

Before Post could react, Garrett threw herself at him and slapped him across the face.

"Leave me alone!" she yelled.

Post turned toward her, his face stinging from the blow.

"Hey, lady, it's lucky we came by," a stocky man snickered. His shirtsleeves were rolled up to expose his muscled arms.

"He bothering you?" a second sailor asked.

"Not anymore!" She shoved her way past the men.

There was laughter behind her as she left. Garrett walked briskly down the corridor, hoping she had managed to keep the true reason for her meeting with Post a secret.

31

Senior Radioman Post knew it would be his only chance to alert the Navy of the *Oklahoma*'s position. It would be very risky, but it had to be done. The number of men lying in their bunks sick increased each day and he had overheard the captain planning a missile strike mounted by the submarine.

With the minimal crew at duty in the conn, Post had been able to alter the instruments so that the inertial fix was obviously wrong.

If the captain is going to mount a strike, Post thought, he will have to resurface to get a precise positional fix in order to ensure the warheads' accuracy. And that would give Post the chance he needed.

Later that day the captain conducted a careful sweep of the area, first with the BXR-19 Top Hat sonar, then with the multipurpose antenna group and finally the periscope. After detecting no nearby communications or any sign of ships, the USS *Oklahoma* surfaced in Gould Bay.

The sea was calm, despite an ugly storm cloud that hovered over the shore. The captain ordered the communications mast extended for a positional check on the

NAVSTAR; the satellite would allow them to determine their exact location to within a few feet so they could reset the inertial fix. This would insure the utmost accuracy for the submarine's missile launch.

"We're still receiving an ELF radio message with our call sign—XB6," Senior Radioman Post told the captain, referring to the extremely low-frequency signal used to communicate simple messages to American submarines.

"We'll ignore the ELF prompt for the time being," Captain Miller replied. "We don't want to give them a chance to secure a fix on us. It's risky enough using the NAVSTAR. So power down your transmitter, Post; we won't be using it today."

"Yes, sir."

Then Captain Miller turned away to speak to Dodd, but from the corner of his eye, the skipper saw the senior radioman key his transmitter.

"What did you do just then?" the captain asked.

"Nothing, sir," Post replied defensively, switching off the transmitter. The hot printer noisily started zipping off characters.

"Damn you!" the captain screamed. "You've sent our call sign on the UHF. And they've signaled back. You've given us away!"

The pistol was in the captain's hand before the radio officer could even react. Miller fired three shots at point-blank range.

"Damn commie traitor," Captain Miller muttered, reholstering his pistol. The sailors around him were silent, unsure how to react. *"You* are now the senior radioman," Miller told the startled man sitting at the radio console.

"Yes, sir," the man said haltingly.

"Now, you two, remove Post's body."

"Aye, aye, Captain," the two sailors said, looking hesitantly at each other.

"Dive!" the captain shouted. "Fifty meters, ahead two-thirds."

The captain retreated to his stateroom for a few minutes to use the head and to fish two more aspirin from the nearly empty bottle on his desk. He closed his eyes and tried to concentrate on what he was planning, then returned to the conn.

As the *Oklahoma* started to dive, the captain stepped toward his communications officer. "Decode the message. We might as well see the disinformation Post sacrificed his life for. Inform me of any more ELF alerts—our call letters or any others."

The communications officer hammered the keys of the cipher machine, sending the decoded message to the printer. The machine clattered noisily. When it was finished, the captain ripped the sheet from the decoder and read it.

TOP SECRET
FR: COMSUBLANT
TO: USS OKLAHOMA
1. REPORT TO NEAREST PORT IMMEDIATELY AT BEST SPEED.
2. BE PREPARED FOR PARANOID BEHAVIOR OF ANY OR ALL CREW MEMBERS.
3. DO NOT, REPEAT NOT, ENGAGE AND DE-STROY ANY OTHER VESSELS OR ACTIVATE ANY WEAPONS SYSTEMS.

4. CONTACT AS SOON AS POSSIBLE FOR FUR-
   THER INSTRUCTIONS.

Captain Miller studied the dispatch for a minute, then thrust it at Dodd.

Dodd read it carefully, then handed it back to the captain.

Miller wadded it and tossed it into a trash bin. He glanced at Dodd, "Same garbage Pageler was beating us over the head with."

"After reading that"—Dodd nodded—"there's no doubt in my mind. They're all using the same story to try to get us to port."

"They have to be working together." Miller nodded. "They'd have to be to have their stories coordinated like that."

"What's our next move, Skipper?"

"Come to my stateroom," Miller ordered, glancing suspiciously at the crew members sitting and working around him. They seemed to be at their assigned tasks, but the captain now suspected everyone of eavesdropping.

Dodd nodded. They couldn't be too careful, not after Dr. Pageler and the senior radio officer had both proven to be spies. Dodd followed the captain forward through the control room, into his stateroom.

Captain Miller washed his hands in the sink, then checked the instrument repeaters showing their course and speed. Satisfied that everything was as it should be, he spoke to Dodd.

The executive officer turned pale as he heard his captain's plan.

32

"Hold your fire!" O.T. roared over the wind a split second after the soldier had jumped from around the front of the MH-60K.

The Delta trooper covering the four helicopter crewmen blinked in the heavy snowfall. "Damn!" he said. "We thought they'd got you when we saw your chopper go down over here. Boy, is Lieutenant Victor ever gonna be glad to see you. Here," he handed Oz a spare magazine of ammunition. "The base is clear if you want to make your way back. We're mopping up the last of the Soviets now while we can still see. I think we've about got 'em all."

Oz snapped the new magazine into his weapon as the soldier vanished back into the storm.

"Boy," O.T. said, "I don't think my heart could've taken much more suspense!"

Oz grinned as he cycled a round into his carbine. "You and Luger get back to the base," he told O.T., his voice all business. "Death Song and I are going to try to raise McTavish or the closest COMSAT on the radio. We need to let them know what's going on."

"I'd rather stay here," O.T. said, shifting from foot

to foot in an effort to warm up. "Some of these AKs lying in the snow must have ammunition in them. You could concentrate on radioing while I watch for trouble."

"That's true," Luger piped up. "We'll guard the chopper while you two work on the radio."

"All right," Oz agreed grudgingly. "Round up some weapons and take your positions inside. You'll freeze if you stay out here. We'll be as quick as we can."

After the four had climbed back into the grounded helicopter, Death Song activated the radio. It proved to be impossible to reach the McTavish Station because of the storm. The navigator then tried to reach one of the communications satellites in an orbit that permitted use as far south as Antarctica.

"I think I've got it," Death Song finally announced after his fifth try to reach the satellite. "I'm not sure how long we can communicate through this snowstorm, though. The junk in the air is really degrading the signal. There's the interrogative code."

The helicopter's computerized radio gave its answering code. There was a short burst of static, and then the radio was on a clear channel waiting to relay their message via the COMSAT to the US Army Command in the US.

"This is Grim One from Anderson Station, calling for Mother Hen, over," Oz spoke slowly into his mike.

"Grim One—" The voice communication ended and there was static.

"Say again, over."

"Grim One, one moment. We'll relay you to Mother Hen."

A few seconds later: "This is Mother Hen. We

heard through McTavish that you were under attack, then we lost contact with McTavish in the storm. What's going on down there? Over."

Oz quickly explained what had happened.

"Listen, Grim One. We have big problems here as well. We know where the *Oklahoma* is—we received a burst message from one of their radio operators who's apparently unaffected by the disease. Our two destroyers, the *Patrick Henry* and *Thomas Jefferson,* both continued northward after you left them. The conventional wisdom was that the sub would be headed toward Cuba, Nicaragua, or even the US. Instead, it's sitting at Gould Bay. But now we don't have anything anywhere close. Do you copy? Over."

"We're reading you. What is the sub doing at Gould Bay? Over."

"That had us guessing for a while. Then we realized the one advantage that spot has. It's close enough inland that a missile launch could reach all the major bases scattered across Antarctica. They got positional information from the NAVSAT just after we got the fix on them. We're betting they're getting ready to launch.

"The question is," Mother Hen continued, "how soon can you get there? I know you said your choppers were all down and your fuel supply is destroyed. But is there any way, any way at all that you can get something to Gould Bay? It might not take much. CDC calculates that much of the crew of the *Oklahoma* is probably incapacitated or even dead by now. Over."

"The situation isn't good," Oz replied. "We'll see what we can do, but we can't make any promises. If we can patch up one chopper, can you airlift fuel from another station? Over."

"That's a negative. The storm will clear in your area shortly and McTavish should be clear a little after that. But they don't have any choppers there to get the fuel to you. Are you sure there are no other sources of fuel there? Over."

"We'll see what we can do. Let me do some checking and we'll get back to you. In the meantime if you can give us any information on where the Soviet soldiers came from, it would help. We don't know what to expect. Over."

"I think we have a line on your Soviets. We started doing some checking after your first radio message to McTavish. There's a small base, Soyez III, close by. One of the members of Anderson Station wasn't accounted for . . . It's possible he might have infected the Soviet base. At any rate Army Intelligence suggests there're only three to four platoons of Soviets based there. It sounds like most of their force must have been involved in the attack. The State Department is getting in touch with Moscow now. Over."

"In that case, that may be one problem we won't have to worry about," Oz said. "The Delta troops seem to have pretty well mopped up. We'll get back to you as soon as we take stock of what we have. Over."

"Talk to you later, Grim One. Over and out."

Death Song switched off the radio and turned to Oz, "And just *how* are we going to get this MH-60K back into the air?"

"I don't know if we can pull it off. But there's one way we might do it." With that, Oz opened his door and leapt into the snowstorm.

33

The weapons officer sat at one of the computer terminals aboard the USS *Oklahoma*, waiting for the captain to speak. Captain Miller stood behind the officer, hand resting on the pistol at his side, his eyes gazing at the bulkhead.

"Ready, Captain," the weapons officer said hesitantly.

Miller's eyes focused on the man, and then on the blank monitor in front of him with its blinking prompt sign.

"Skipper?" Dodd asked.

"I'm fine," the captain replied wearily. "All right. Type 'system.' "

The weapons officer carefully typed as the captain dictated. The word "SYSTEM" appeared on the screen before them and on the tactical/navigation display in the control room. A moment later an "OK" appeared. The computer was awaiting other commands.

Captain Miller gave another string of code words to the weapons officer who typed them in. The captain paused, then continued: "Arm sequence."

"ARM SEQUENCE" was typed. There was a momentary delay on the computer screen and then "READY" appeared on the screen followed by "VERIFY."

"Arm Trident IIs."

"TEST?" the computer screen flashed after the weapons officer had typed in the captain's command.

"No test," the captain whispered.

"SYSTEM UP," appeared on the display. Then a warning flashed on the screen, "WARNING: COMMAND DECISION IS NOT MONITORED. OPERATIONAL CODE: WEAPONS OFFICER?"

The weapons officer swallowed, then typed in his code. The letters he typed were represented on the screen only as a series of asterisks rather than the letters and numbers he actually entered into the computer.

"VERIFIED," the screen read. "OPERATIONAL CODE: ENGINEERING OFFICER?"

The weapons officer rose and the engineering officer sat down at the keyboard. He hesitated, then started typing rapidly.

"ERROR," the screen read. "OPERATIONAL CODE: ENGINEERING OFFICER?"

"Damn it, don't screw it up," the captain said angrily, his hand again snaking toward his pistol.

"Sorry," the engineering officer said. "This headache . . ."

"Get on with it."

The man typed, more slowly this time.

"VERIFIED," the screen answered. The computer continued by asking in turn for the verification code of Dodd and the captain. Both men entered their secret codes of letters and numbers. These were followed by another series of interrogatives from the computer asking for code words that each of the officers gave to the machine.

Finally, the captain had the weapons officer enter the commands allowing targeting information to be uploaded into the computer for the Trident II missiles. That done, the operational program was modified so each missile could be armed and launched separately on the captain's command.

In a short time the computer screen dropped back into its standard mode and the tactical/navigational display returned to normal in the control room.

"It's done," the weapons officer whispered, wiping the sweat from his forehead as he turned to the captain.

"Good," Miller replied. "Now, Mr. Dodd, take us in as close as we can get to the shore."

34

Working with the Delta Team and using several snow tractors, Sergeant Marvin and his ground crew had managed to shove and pull the remaining MH-60K through the snowstorm and into one of the sheds at the perimeter of Anderson Station. In the meantime Oz and a detachment of the American troops had improvised a bucket brigade that toiled in the blizzard to relay fuel siphoned from the downed Mi-6 Hook helicopter to the shed where the MH-60K rested.

"I just don't know if it will hold," Sergeant Marvin told Oz, wiping his face with an oil-covered hand.

"We don't need a written guarantee," Oz said, his breath fogging up in front of him in the poorly heated dome where Marvin and his ground crew were frantically working to repair the damage done to the helicopter. "Just so the fuel tanks last long enough for us to get there."

"I'm not even able to promise you that," Marvin said, shaking his head.

"Well, I'm more worried about this crud than the chopper," O.T. said as he laid the last can of fuel that had been drained from the Mi-6 Hook on the floor of the shed. "You sure this stuff will burn in an American chopper?"

"That I'm sure of," Marvin said. "I suspect you could run this helicopter on cheap perfume."

"I had a date like that once," O.T. smirked.

Sergeant Marvin's crew continued to toil over the MH-60K after it had been refueled, checking control linkages and repairing the minor damage caused during its combat and forced landing wherever they could.

"It's too bad we couldn't salvage much of the ammunition or any of the rockets," Marvin told Oz. "We could only scrounge a partial belt for your dual machine guns."

"You've worked a miracle getting all this together in just a few hours," Oz said. "Besides, if what we have in mind works, we shouldn't need any weapons on the MH-60K. We owe you and your team a lot."

Marvin shrugged. "We didn't figure we could afford to wait around if that sub is about to nuke us. Besides, the chopper hasn't got you there yet. Thank me if and when you make it to your destination."

Oz slapped Marvin on the back and turned as the side door to the shed opened, letting in a gust of cold air and snow.

"Looks like the storm is breaking," Dr. Shahid told Oz as she entered the shed. "Here," she said, handing an empty cup to Oz. She set the thermos she carried on a tool-covered table, carefully removed the container's lid, then turned and poured coffee into the cup Oz held.

"Thanks," Oz said, nestling the cup in his cold hands.

"Are they making any progress with your helicopter?" Shahid asked.

Oz nodded, studying Shahid's face for a moment. "With a little luck, we just might make it."

"Oz," Death Song called from the side door of the helicopter. "I've reached McTavish."

"Good," Oz yelled. "Be there in a minute." He turned back toward Shahid. "Excuse me. And thanks for the coffee."

Shahid said nothing, but flashed a quick smile at Oz.

Oz crossed to the helicopter and scrambled through the pilot's door. The instrument panel was lit up, casting an eerie glow on Death Song's face.

"Let's see if McTavish can get what we'll need," Oz told Death Song.

35

The MH-60K sputtered to a start and lifted shakily into the air. Oz cautiously pushed the pedals in the cockpit, causing the chopper to face the tail of the storm.

Oz stared through the side window of the helicopter at the men down below who waved to the helicopter. His eyes scanned the crowd until he spied Shahid, standing in her white fur coat. O.T. and Luger stood next to her, since they wouldn't be needed for the risky mission Oz had planned.

Death Song tapped a button to the side of his VSD (Vertical Situation Display); the helicopter's computer plotted the course to McTavish.

Oz checked the coordinates, and then pointed the helicopter onto course. He pushed the control column forward, heading for the station at a near maximum speed of 180 miles per hour.

An hour and a half later Oz and Death Song had overtaken the storm. One of the main tanks had started leaking again and the helicopter had nearly exhausted its fuel.

"McTavish, this is NS-1," Oz called, for what seemed to be the hundredth time. "Over."

"NS-1, this is—" the signal was broken by static, garbling the message.

"Say again. Over."

"NS-1, this is McTavish. Washington has informed us of the urgency of your mission and has given us the go-ahead with your idea. We'll help you however we can. Over."

"Thanks, McTavish," Oz told them. "We're headed for your base but are experiencing a leak in our fuel tank. We're going to get as close to you as possible, but we'll be going down before we reach you. Our ETA for emergency landing is five minutes. That will put us about five to ten miles west of you. Over."

"The storm seems to be clearing here, NS-1, but I'm afraid we don't have any helicopters at the base now, except for the CONCOP with the bugs in its control system. Both our choppers are stuck at Siple Station and will probably be grounded by the storm at least until tomorrow. We *will* have all our available snow tractors searching for you as soon as possible. Stay on the line so you can give us your precise coordinates. Over."

"Your search parties will be much appreciated. Over and out."

Oz managed to land the MH-60K before its fuel was depleted. The chopper sat buried to its doors in a drift of snow that glittered in the bright sunlight.

The two Night Stalkers waited impatiently.

Finally, Death Song spotted one of the search parties. "There's a snow tractor," he exclaimed, pointing to a hill in the west.

"Collect your rifle and let's go meet them," Oz said. "We don't have any time to waste."

The pilot and navigator left their grounded helicopter, rifles in hand, and climbed through the deep snow toward the snow tractor that was racing to meet them.

Members of the MH-60K ground crews left behind at McTavish stood on the tarmac. Oz and Death Song leapt from the snow tractor and jogged to the CONCOP that sat waiting for them.

"The CONCOP is fueled and ready to go as per your instructions, sir," a member of the ground crew reported to Oz. The crewman helped Oz into the cramped rear cockpit of the aircraft. "The manufacturer has been running diagnostics at their plant in the U.S. But they still haven't come up with anything about the glitch. The Army's officially grounded all the CONCOPs. Are you sure you want to fly it?"

"It's the only hope we have." Oz settled into the seat and snapped the harness around himself as Death Song climbed into the seat in front of him.

"All weapons systems are in place and functional," the ground crewman related, stepping back. "We checked them just before you got here."

"Thanks," Oz said.

"Good luck, sir."

Oz gave the man a thumbs-up signal and closed the canopy.

I have a feeling we'll be needing a lot of luck, Oz thought as he started the engine on the CONCOP.

36

The dead mechanic's body was almost on Major Churkin Novikov's polished boot. The bodies of the mechanic's crew lay next to him, their blood soaking into the snow. A thin curl of smoke rose from the barrel of the major's AKR.

Novikov paced toward the next frightened man trembling on his knees. "And did you manage to get your Hind-D ready for takeoff as I ordered?" the major demanded, centering the carbine's muzzle on the man's forehead.

"Yes, sir. It . . . It is ready for your soldiers."

"Good. We'll have you stand by in case you're mistaken." The major turned to the next mechanic.

The man spit at the major's boots.

Before the spittle had hardly landed, the AKR blazed, slaughtering the mechanic and his crew of three. Major Novikov took a moment to pick the best eight men from the troops aligned behind him: "You, and you, and you . . ." He marched along the line. "Get aboard the Hind-D," he growled. The Spetsnaz troops saluted smartly and double-timed their way to the heavily armed Hind-D.

The major turned and walked to the soldier standing beside the Mi-28 Havoc that Novikov had managed to land at Soyez III. "Are you ready?" he asked his new pilot.

"Yes, sir. The helicopter is refueled and the weapons replenished."

"The storm has passed. Let's get started."

"Yes, sir."

Major Novikov climbed into the gunship and slammed the canopy closed.

"This time!" he promised himself. He didn't have much, but the Americans had to be low on ammunition as well as manpower. And the major knew they were low on fuel—he had destroyed the supply dump himself. This time Anderson Station would be his.

Grace Garrett's nose was assaulted by the smell of putrefaction as she cautiously stepped from the narrow metal corridor of the submarine into the crowded sick bay. Six bunks had been set up in the room; two now held men that were obviously dead. In the corner, leaning against the body bags containing stiff corpses, the ship's only surviving medic lay in a deep slumber brought on by exhaustion.

Tiptoeing past the medic, Garrett reached into the tall metal storage cabinet that was standing open, its keys hanging from the lock in the door. After searching a few moments, she located a vial of penicillin and a disposable hypodermic syringe still in its wrapper.

Garrett crossed to a gurney where Squad Leader Adams lay unconscious. For a moment Garrett thought the man was dead, but then she saw the slight rise of his chest. After glancing toward the medic to be sure he was still asleep, she carefully unwrapped the syringe, guessed at the dosage, and pumped air from the hypodermic into the vial.

After the hypodermic had been filled to half its capacity, she extracted the needle. She put the vial into the pocket of her jumpsuit and then positioned the needle over Adams's thigh. Garrett hesitated a moment and then jabbed the needle through the fabric of his uniform into his thigh muscle.

Adams gave a low moan and then became quiet when the needle was extracted from his leg.

Garrett looked around and spied two more marines lying in the bunks. She repeated the procedure, wondering if she was giving the shots properly and if the dosage was large enough—or too large. Had she helped, or had she actually done something that would hasten their deaths?

I'll just have to hope, she thought, sneaking from the sick bay.

37

The CONCOP rushed through the dazzling, cloudless sky. Oz had stopped worrying about the possibility of the CONCOP's computer glitch occurring again. They were taking a nap-of-the-earth trip with the TF/TA system controlling their flight. As low and as fast as they were flying, one glitch and both Oz and Death Song would be dead before they were even aware of the failure.

Oz monitored the instruments while the black chopper guided itself aloft, flitting above the snow-covered hill and then dropping downward, giving the riders the sensation of free-falling for several seconds. The rotors above the fuselage were tilted forward for maximum speed and purred as they cut through the frigid Antarctic air.

Death Song studied his instrument display. "We've got company ahead of us. Two birds . . . Look like choppers. They're flying very low and very fast. Must be military."

Oz studied the ice ahead of them. "I don't see them."

"Directly in front of us."

Oz strained to see the two specks in the distance. "Let's arm the weapons."

"Weapons armed," Death Song announced.

"You retain control of the machine gun. Give me the rockets."

"Yes, sir," Death Song replied.

"The rear one looks like a Hind-D," Death Song said moments later. "The other must be a Havoc. Their present course will deliver them directly to Anderson Station."

"Must be the last of the detachment at Soyez III," Oz said.

"They've got nothing good in mind, that's for sure—both choppers are carrying rockets. Shall we take them or sit tight?"

Oz thought a moment. They couldn't afford to waste time or ammunition. But if they went directly for the submarine, it was likely the Soviets would detect them and pursue. While the CONCOP could outrun both Russian helicopters, the chances of being picked off by the Havoc's missiles were good. Besides, he didn't like the idea of letting the Soviets attack Anderson Station again.

So we'll fight, Oz decided. "Let's see if we can get them in a quick pass. We'll stay low, then pop up to get a clear shot with our rockets. Let's save the Hellfires for the submarine. Use them only if we can't avoid getting clipped without them."

"We're getting in range for the Hind-D," Death Song told him. "They still haven't detected us."

"I'll head on in."

Oz watched his FLIR as he climbed into the air and

then brought the helicopter into a shallow dive, its nose pointing toward the Hind-D.

"Firing," Oz advised Death Song. Oz held the helicopter ahead of them on target as an unguided rocket hissed from its pod to his right, making a fiery arc as it jetted toward the Hind-D. A cross wind caught the missile, throwing it wide of its mark.

"Firing two more," Oz said. He again held the CONCOP on target, aiming downwind so the missiles would be turned toward the target by the wind blowing on their fins.

This time the missiles darted toward the Soviet helicopter, curving to the side to collide with the chopper's tail and the rear engine cowling. The aircraft tore apart with the twin explosions, then burst into flames as the fuel ignited. The wreckage tumbled across the ice below as the CONCOP flashed over it, sweeping the dark smoke coming from it into swirling patterns.

"The Havoc's slowing," Death Song warned. "We're overshooting them."

His warning came too late. The CONCOP raced by as the Soviet chopper dawdled close to the ground.

Once the Americans passed, the Mi-28 Havoc leapt into the air to follow them. Major Novikov sat in the front cockpit of the helicopter. As the American machine tore past, he locked his missile-launch radar onto the CONCOP.

"He's locked onto us," Death Song warned as his instruments beeped a warning. "Better take evasive measures."

Oz forced the helicopter into a climb and then rolled it to the right.

Novikov thumbed the control in his helicopter.

His missile sped from the pylon toward the American helicopter.

Death Song released a flare that dropped from an internal countermeasures compartment built into the fuselage of the CONCOP. The missile wandered and then locked onto the flare while Oz continued his turn and climbed to the right.

The Soviet missile caught up with the flare and detonated, sounding like distant thunder inside the American chopper.

"They're still on our tail," Death Song advised.

Oz continued to pull on the collective pitch lever, taking them into the steepest possible climb.

The Soviet Havoc followed, unable to match the CONCOP's speed and rate of ascent. The Americans climbed higher and higher.

"I'm going to try looping this thing," Oz said. "I know it's possible." It's just that I've never done it before, he added to himself.

But before Oz had time to execute the difficult maneuver, the computer started its vocal alarm: "Warning: you are exceeding the flight speed of the helicopter. Warning: you are exceeding the flight speed of the helicopter—"

Oz snapped the alarm off.

"Hang on," the pilot warned Death Song a moment after he felt the control column go limp in his hand.

The USS *Oklahoma* smelled of death and sweat.

Dodd was relieved to get the submarine into position. There were barely enough crewmen to operate the helm and engines. The executive officer sluggishly reached for the intercom and snapped it on. "Captain Miller?"

"Who is it?"

"Dodd, Captain. We're in position for the launch."

"Good. I'll be there in a little while. I need to rest."

"Captain, if we don't launch soon, we're not going to have the manpower to continue to operate. Weapons Officer Newton is barely conscious and—"

"I'll be there. Quit your whining."

38

The CONCOP continued its rapid climb, completely out of control.

"Control column's dead again," Oz cautioned Death Song. "I'm going to try stopping and starting the engine. Damn, they need to issue parachutes with this thing . . . Cutting power to the engine."

The engine stopped. The only sound was the wind whistling on the surface of the CONCOP. With the loss of power, the helicopter stopped its ascent, leveled, and started to plunge downward.

Oz tried to ignore the Soviet chopper as it altered its flight to match that of the Americans.

Oz endeavored to restart the engine.

Nothing.

Now the icy hills below started racing up to meet them.

Oz tried the engine again. It abruptly thundered to life, fighting to gain control of the blades that were being whipped by the air speeding through them.

The controls came alive in Oz's hands. He eased the collective pitch lever upward and brought back the control column, wondering if the torque produced by the rushing air would rip the rotors apart.

"Come on . . ." he muttered as they neared the ground.

The Havoc behind him fired a burst from its cannon. The heavy bullets cut under the Americans, barely missing them.

The rotors made a buckling sound that filled the cockpit, and the rate of the CONCOP's descent decreased. The machine thundered to a halt meters above the ice. They skimmed close to the snow, then started to climb.

"They're getting positioned to lock onto us again with their missiles," Death Song warned.

"I'm trying to loop," Oz notified Death Song. The American pilot twisted in his seat trying to locate the Havoc pursuing them. There! Right on our tail, he thought. He lifted the collective pitch lever, taking the CONCOP into a steep climb.

The Soviet chopper followed, Novikov still trying to fire his missiles at the Americans. A beeper warned Oz that the Havoc's missile-control radar had locked onto the CONCOP.

The American chopper continued to climb until it was ascending vertically and the Havoc lost the target on its screen.

"Hang on," Oz warned Death Song.

The CONCOP continued upward, losing speed and threatening to stall. And then the two Americans hung in their straps, upside down. The helicopter seemed to creep in the air as the blood rushed to Oz's head. Then the chopper started to drop.

Oz came out of the maneuver with a minimum of

trouble, dropping behind the Mi-28 Havoc that now sat exposed below them.

"We're right on target," Death Song said.

Oz's little finger poised on the fire button of the control column.

The four rockets Oz released shot forward on their tails of flame. For a moment they seemed off-course as the CONCOP continued to drop toward the Havoc. Then the rockets struck. The Mi-28 Havoc blew apart, spraying across the ice far below.

Oz lifted his helicopter from its speedy descent. "Now what's the course for Gould Bay?" he asked, all emotion drained from his voice.

"Here you go," Death Song told Oz as he punched up the map display.

Oz aligned the CONCOP onto the new course heading, dropping toward the surface below them. "Switching to TF/TA so we can go in low. I hope we can make it in time."

Minutes later the CONCOP was climbing a low mountain of ice. The chopper hurtled above the slopes in a giddy fall that took them toward the hills in front of the icy bay on the other side of the peaks.

"There's Gould Bay," Death Song exclaimed.

The TF/TA radar automatically hauled the CON-COP into a tight climb, skimming the hills covered with hoarfrost that glimmered in the intense sunlight.

Oz shut off the TF/TA; the helicopter shuddered slightly, switching to manual flight, and for a terrible moment Oz thought the controls were failing again. When he realized they hadn't failed, he took a deep breath and then spoke: "Any sign of the submarine?"

"No," Death Song replied. He scanned the helicopter's instrument display. "No radio or radar signals, either."

"Let's try Mother Hen. I'm circling the bay."

"I'll have the COMSAT in a second."

Oz brought the helicopter around, searching the ice below. He spied a round, broken section of the ice, then noticed the nearly straight channel that had been cut by the icebreaker.

"The satellite is interrogating our computer for the access code," Death Song disclosed. "Okay. You can go ahead now."

Oz triggered the radio switch on the control column, "NS-1 calling for Mother Hen. Over."

"This is Mother Hen. Go ahead, NS-1. Over."

"We're at Gould Bay in the CONCOP. But there's no sign of our target. Over."

"They'll undoubtedly launch from underwater. What kind of armament do you have? Over."

"We have four Hellfires, a handful of rockets, and a twenty-two caliber Minigun. We're talking David against Goliath here. Over."

The radio was silent for a moment, and then Mother Hen replied, "There're two tactics that might work. They're both long shots, but that's all we have."

"We're all ears, Mother Hen."

Mother Hen described the two tactics the chopper could try.

One was to fire their missiles and rockets into the ice alongside the channel through which the *Oklahoma* would launch the Tridents. This would make enough large ice fragments in the water that the submarine would be forced to surface to fire its missiles or risk hav-

ing them damaged during launch. But no one thought
this would be practical with only four Hellfires and
2.75-inch rockets, even if the submarine's exact position were known.

They elected to use the second tactic, although it
too offered only a marginal chance for success.

Oz flew the helicopter along the channel that had
been cut through the ice by the icebreaker. The open
water in the channel was a mirrored aquamarine line
running through a sea of white ice. The pilot knew that
somewhere under the tranquil water, a submarine was
about to unleash 192 warheads at the bases spread
across the southernmost continent.

"We're on top of the coordinates that Mother Hen
gave as the shallowest practical depth the *Oklahoma*
could reach," Death Song told Oz.

"I'll circle the area. Let's hope Mother Hen's tacti-
cians were right in their assumption that the submarine
headed up the channel as far as it could to gain maximum range. Are our weapons systems still armed?"

"Roger. They're hot."

Oz brought the helicopter into its second circle of
the area.

"Wait a minute," Death Song said. "West at
eleven o'clock. Look at the channel with your FLIR.
There's a difference in the temperature. The sub's reactor must be heating the water."

Oz retracted the FLIR from his helmet so it covered his right eye. "Yeah, I see it. I'll hover next to the
spot. If nothing happens in a few minutes, we'll have
to land or risk running out of fuel. Are you ready?"

"Yeah. I hope Mother Hen knew what they were

talking about when it comes time to stop the missiles.
I've never heard of anybody trying to do this before."

"That's because the subs aren't supposed to be
launching when someone's right beside them."

Captain Miller and Executive Officer Dodd lifted
the weapons officer into his chair.

"Don't crap out on us now," the captain told the
sick man. "It's time to launch. Here, I'll get your
key—"

"I've got it," the man hissed in a low voice. He
reached to the console and stuck his key into the lock
guarding the nuclear-launch console. "Ready?" he
asked Dodd.

Dodd hunched over the other end of the console
with his key in the lock. "Ready."

"Okay. On three. One . . . Two . . . Three."

The two men twisted the keys.

"Captain," Dodd said. "We're ready to launch."

"Open tube one and fire," the captain ordered.

The weapons officer's shaking hand reached for
the controls.

"Here comes the first one!" Oz yelled.

The water five hundred meters in front of the helicopter boiled as a missile was forced from its tube on
a column of compressed air. The white missile vaulted
into the air, hanging on the tall fountain a moment before its rocket engine crackled to life.

Death Song fired a Hellfire as the Trident II rocket
rose from the water. The laser designator tracked the
rocket as Death Song kept his eye on it. Then the missile accelerated; the Hellfire missed.

The Trident II gathered speed, rising on a plume of smoke. Within seconds the SLBM was out of range for the Hellfire missiles. The Hellfire exploded harmlessly on the ice beyond the channel.

"Damn!" Death Song cried.

"Settle down," Oz ordered. "We got twenty-three more to worry about."

"But that one missile carried enough warheads to—"

"Get it out of your mind. That's an order. We've got to concentrate on what we're doing. Give me the rocket pod while you keep the Hellfires. That's what we should have done in the first place."

"All right," Death Song said, struggling to control his emotions. "You've got the rockets. I'm retaining control of the three remaining Hellfires."

"Missile one is off," the weapons officer announced in a hoarse whisper.

"Sonar to conn."

"What is it?" the captain asked his sonar officer.

"We registered an explosion on the ice about a half mile from us," Sonar Chief Thompson said. "It came moments after the missile launch."

"It wasn't caused by the missile?" the captain asked.

"No, Skipper. Someone set off an explosion of some type."

"We'll have to ignore it." The captain turned to his weapons officer. "Open launch tube two. Fire Two."

"Firing Two."

*　　*　　*

The water in front of the CONCOP again boiled as a second missile shot from its tube. The Trident II rose on the explosion of compressed air. The white missile then hung briefly in the atmosphere. Its engine came to life with an explosive burst of flame.

Death Song fired a Hellfire as the Trident II rose; simultaneously, Oz shot a single rocket from the pod alongside him. The laser designator slaved to Death Song's helmet tracked the Trident as the navigator kept his eye on it; Oz's rocket sped toward the missile.

The Trident accelerated and the Hellfire connected, followed by the rocket Oz had launched. The huge Trident II wobbled briefly, and then the fuel burning inside it jetted through the hole blasted in the side of the missile. The Trident lifted in a wide spiral, its engine making a low-pitched crackling as it superheated the air it traveled through. The Trident II's course curved, pointing it downward toward the ice. It continued its descent, circling with greater speed.

Oz held his breath as the Trident missile dropped across the top of the *Oklahoma*. There was a muffled explosion as the missile hit the water. The burning wreckage was lifted back into the air, tiny fragments tumbling across the ice. The larger chunks of wreckage dropped back in nearly the same spot from which the missile had left the water.

"Mother Hen was right," Oz almost whispered. "The fail-safe didn't allow the warheads to go off. Let's get ready for the next launch."

Almost at the instant the second Trident II had blasted from its tube by the compressed air, Captain

Miller had given his next order. "Open tube three. Fire Three!"

There was an explosion as the second Trident II was hit by Oz and Death Song's rockets. Tube three opened as the wreckage of the second Trident dropped into the water.

The captain watched his weapons officer launch the third Trident. Rather than the normal shudder of the SLBM being propelled upward by the compressed air, there was a jarring thump as the wreckage of the second held the third in its tube for a moment. Then the third missile broke free.

But the missile failed to rise from the water. It dropped back on the tubes, creating a massive thud that rang through the corridors inside the sub and damaged several of the tube doors. Moments later the rocket's fail-safe disconnected its engine to prevent its igniting on top of the submarine.

"Rocket three, failure to fire," the weapons officer told the captain. "I think the second rocket has also tumbled back onto us. I'm registering damage in tubes three, four, six, twelve, and fourteen through twenty-four."

"You can't trick me!" the captain shrieked. "Launch all rockets. Now." He held his pistol in a shaky hand.

The weapons officer turned wearily. "That can't be done, Skipper—"

Miller raised his pistol.

"Hold it right there, Skipper," Adams's voice called from the hatchway leading from the conn.

Captain Miller turned to see Squad Leader Adams

step through the hatchway, M16 rifle at his shoulder, its muzzle leveled at Miller.

The captain hesitated, then swung his pistol toward the marine entering the conn.

Adams fired a single, carefully aimed shot. The slug struck the captain in the forearm, ripping a hole as it exited. Blood and flesh splattered across the radio console behind Miller as the bullet shattered a dial on its face.

The captain's pistol dropped from his senseless hand and clattered onto the metal deck. Miller remained on his feet, grasping the bloody hole in his arm as he glared at the marine.

"Don't anyone else move," Adams ordered as the men in the conn tensed on the edge of their seats. "Mr. Dodd, surface," he ordered. "It's time we set everything right. If we still can."

Dodd hesitated.

"Surface!"

The executive officer waited a fraction of a second, then gave the order to surface.

Oz and Death Song watched as the *Oklahoma*'s sail emerged from the ocean. The submarine stopped its ascent for a few minutes as it drew air through its snorkel tube and pumped its ballast tanks empty. The water was expelled and the submarine rose, lifting the wreckage of the Trident II rockets that littered the missile launch deck.

"*Oklahoma*, this is US Army helicopter CONCOP-1. Come in, please."

"I'm not sure they can read us," Death Song told

Oz. "Their radio mast looks pretty beat up from the rocket debris."

"Let's keep trying," Oz replied. *"Oklahoma,* this is US Army helicopter CONCOP-1. Come in, please," he repeated.

There was a long pause. Oz waited, wondering if anyone on the ship was capable of making any sort of logical decision, let alone answering their message.

The radio seemed dead.

"Well, one thing's for sure: they won't be launching any more missiles," Death Song said over the intercom. "Look at those tubes."

Oz lifted the helicopter over the rear of the submarine. The damage to each tube was obvious. None of the Tridents could possibly be operational.

"Connect us to the COMSAT again," the pilot ordered Death Song.

After contacting Mother Hen, Oz explained what had happened. "We're only sorry we didn't manage to stop the first Trident," Oz finally said.

"You'll be glad to know that the Trident II didn't function properly," Mother Hen came back to him. "The SLBM went through the correct ballistic arch but the warheads failed to deploy. We'll be searching for those warheads for years to come, I suspect. This is the first time the Pentagon's been happy about a Trident failure since they started testing the prototypes. At any rate no *working* warheads got past you guys. You did a good job.

"In the meantime ETA for the three C-5As landing at McTavish is in fifteen minutes," Mother Hen told Oz. "We can't land them close to you, but we can have troops parachute in. They'll have the explosives necessary to knock out the sub. Over."

"Mother Hen, I don't think that's necessary," Oz radioed back. "The sub is so heavily damaged that it isn't going anywhere. In fact, I'm not sure it will still be afloat by the time they assemble the choppers and bring the troops in from McTavish. Over."

"Okay," Mother Hen agreed. "We'll route everyone on the C-5As to McTavish and ferry the troops to your position on the Black Hawks the transports are carrying. They'll arrive in about two hours. In the meantime you'll have to stay alert. Over."

"We're setting down on the ice to conserve fuel," Oz replied. "We'll keep sharp. NS-1, over and out."

A marine and three sailors climbed onto the deck of the submarine and motioned to the CONCOP.

"What do you think?" Death Song asked.

"I wish they weren't armed," Oz answered. "You stay with the helicopter. Take it aloft and attack if you need to. I'll see what they want."

Oz retracted the slide on his Ruger P-85 pistol, then checked to be sure its safety was off before placing it into his flight vest. He cracked open the canopy, unbuckled his harness, and climbed out of the CONCOP.

The snow crunched under his boots as he approached the submarine. The USS *Oklahoma* seemed bigger and blacker up close. He was aware of how the sail towered above the icy plain that was really the surface of the frozen ocean.

The marine stepped toward the edge of the *Oklahoma*'s deck. Oz fought the impulse to reach for his Ruger.

Squad Leader Adams cleared his throat and spoke in a loud voice that, in the cold, quiet air, easily carried across the distance between the two men. "Sir, the captain has been relieved of command. Most of those still sick are confined to quarters. Those of us who have taken antibiotics are in control now. Our radio mast was apparently damaged by the debris so we couldn't radio you after we surfaced. Can you send a message for us?"

"What's the message?" Oz asked.

"Pretty simple." Adams smiled grimly. "For the US Naval Command: The USS *Oklahoma* asks permission to return to the nearest port."

"I'll send it," Oz promised.

"Thank you, sir."

Oz returned the marine's salute and headed for the CONCOP.

E P I L O G U E

The Rangers arrived on their UH-60 Black Hawks an hour after Oz had radioed that things had returned more-or-less to normal on the USS *Oklahoma*. The Rangers helped remove the dead from the submarine and cleaned the debris from its deck.

Oz and Death Song rode back to McTavish Station in a Black Hawk helicopter, leaving the CONCOP to be retrieved by a Sikorsky S-64 Skycrane that was being flown in from Siple Station.

A team from the USSR arrived at Soyez III after a message had been sent to the Soviet government through diplomatic channels. The arriving troops, wearing protective masks, encountered only scattered resistance. The prisoners taken by the soldiers were immediately treated with penicillin and the base decontaminated. Following the takeover of the camp, Dr. Mikhalsky was freed and returned to McTavish where he joined Dr. Grace Garrett, who had left the submarine.

After taking a day to get cleaned and rested, the remnants of the Night Stalkers and Delta Team commenced boarding a C-5A for transport headed to their headquarters in Fort Bragg, North Carolina.

O.T., Oz, Death Song, and Luger trudged the icy tarmac of McTavish Station toward the transport. "So the *Oklahoma* is headed back to sea?" O.T asked.

"That's right," Oz answered. "Three quarters of the crew are dead but the rest recovered after a round of antibiotics. The submarine has enough of a crew to allow her to limp into port." He stopped, glancing toward the central dome of the station. "You guys go on, I'll be there in a minute."

"Okay," O.T. chuckled, eyeing the figure in the white fur coat who was sauntering toward the C-5A. "Don't stay out too late."

Oz turned and ambled back across the tarmac to face Dr. Shahid as she approached. He studied the graceful face ringed by the white fur parka and half hidden by large sunglasses.

"I was hoping I'd catch you before you left," Shahid told him. "The trouble with you strong, silent types is you're always riding into the sunset without saying good-bye . . . Anyway, if you're ever in Atlanta, look me up."

"I'm sure I could be there sometime soon."

"I hope so. Try to stay in touch. Here." She handed him a slip of paper.

Oz glanced at the phone number and then stuck it into a coat pocket. "I'll be seeing you, then," he said, smiling. He turned, crossed to the cargo ramp of the C-5A, and stepped into the belly of the giant plane without looking back.

Shahid watched the plane as it taxied along the runway, her tears hidden by the dark glasses.

Duncan Long is internationally recognized as a fire-arms expert, and has had over twenty books published on that subject, as well as numerous magazine articles. In addition to his nonfiction writing, Long has written a science fiction novel, *Antigrav Unlimited*. He has an MA in music composition, and has worked as a rock musician; he has spent nine years teaching in public schools. Duncan Long lives in eastern Kansas with his wife and two children.